equally yoked

LaureL

shadrach

series

3

equally yoked

stephanie perry moore

MOODY PUBLISHERS
CHICAGO

All Scripture quotations are taken from the King James Version.

Library of Congress Cataloging-in-Publication Data

Moore, Stephanie Perry.
    Equally yoked / by Stephanie Perry Moore.
        p. cm.—(Laurel Shadrach series)
    ISBN 0-8024-4037-1
    I. Title. II. Series.
    PZ7.M788125 Eq 2003

                                                2002015940

                    3 5 7 9 10 8 6 4 2

Printed in the United States of America

For my uncle,
Rev. Cedric Bernard Perry Sr.

I'm so grateful God allowed you
to be my big brother
during my high school years.
You scrutinized my dates
and checked out my friends,
all in an effort to make sure
I hung with the right crowd.
It is my hope that the readers of this novel
will learn the lesson you taught me:
Be yoked with folks who love the Lord.
Thanks for caring.
I am a better person because you were there.

contents

acknowledgments

today was not a good marriage day. My husband and I disagreed on something so insignificant that at the end of the big blowup, I couldn't even tell you what we were arguing about. But gosh, I was mad at him. I honestly wondered how I got stuck with him in the first place. And the feeling was mutual. So if you've ever felt like your best friend was your worst enemy . . . been there, felt that.

I began to pray for help, and the Lord reminded my spirit of what my marriage was built on. God is the solid foundation, the common thread, the One who brought us together. We knew when we married He was the only thing that would hold us together for life. If we didn't have Him, who knows where we'd be?

The same is true, I believe, about every relationship into which a believer enters. If two people who believe in God come together, the God they love can work things out when storms come. But imagine what can happen if the two people are "unequally yoked"—if only one of them has God in his or her heart. Don't get caught up in unnecessary drama because you're hanging with the wrong folks. Choose friends wisely. Make it a prerequisite that anyone who wants to hang out with you has to know God.

My special thanks to everyone who supports my writing: my parents, Franklin and Shirley Perry Sr.; my publishing company, Moody Press, especially Karen Waddles; my reading pool: Laurel Basso, Kathleen Hanson, Sarah Hunter, Carol Shadrach, and Marietta Shadrach; my assistants: Nakia Austin, Shayla Turner, Jami McNair, Rachel Splaine, and Nicole Duncan; my sorority sisters of Delta Sigma Theta, particularly the Stone Mountain-Lithonia Alumnae Chapter; my daughters, Sydni and Sheldyn; my husband, Derrick Moore; and most importantly, my Savior, Jesus Christ. Because you are there, I can do what God has called me to do. I write for Him. Thanks!

beating
the odds

"gosh, you're pretty," Branson said, awakening me.

I sat up in the stiff hospital chair and stared at my ex-boyfriend. His head and chest were wrapped in white gauze, and his hands had tubes sticking out of them. "What time is it?"

"Five-thirty in the afternoon," he informed me.

"Already? I got here at two, saw my brother for like five minutes, then came to see if you were all right. Guess I dozed off."

"I'm glad you came to see me. It shows how much you care."

I got up, stood next to Branson, and held his hand, careful not to disturb the tubes attached to it. "I do. Deeply."

He smiled. It felt good to let out my true feelings.

I'd been on an emotional roller coaster with Branson Price all through the last year of high school. We started out great, but then he wanted to take our relationship further than I wanted to. When I refused to give in, he turned to my best friend, Brittany Cox. They went all the way.

I was angry at him for betraying me. And yet, I could never shake the deep feelings I had for him. Now, even if my dream of marrying Branson ever did come true, I would never be his first.

It wasn't just Branson I got angry with. Brittany and I didn't talk for months. But God reminded me that I was supposed to forgive others as He forgave me. Besides, circumstances in Brittany's life—like her being diagnosed with HIV—had turned my girlfriend into a different person. She'd become really humble. When I finally forgave her, she asked for my forgiveness too. So our friendship started anew.

"How's your brother?" Branson asked. I knew he felt guilty about getting into that car crash the night before. He and his best friend, Bo, had gotten drunk during prom and challenged a bunch of guys from a rival sports team to a race. My brother Lance and another guy piled into Bo's white Chevy Blazer. Moments later, the El Camino they were racing against smashed into the side of a mountain, and the Blazer went over a cliff. The guy in the backseat with Lance got out with just a broken arm. I'd heard the doctor say Branson had suffered a severe concussion and internal bleeding, though it seemed to be under control now. Bo, however, wasn't so lucky. He was still in a coma, and he'd lost all feeling in both of his legs.

"They released Lance this afternoon," I said, "just before I came in here to check on you. He's still a little lightheaded from that gash over his eye. And the stitches will probably leave a scar." *Still, it could be a lot worse,* I wanted to add. But I didn't want to compound Branson's guilt about Bo.

"And where's your boyfriend?" Branson asked.

I looked away and thought about Foster McDowell.

Foster was tall, tan, and gorgeous. He was also a strong Christian and extremely sweet. He played piano beautifully and had an awesome singing voice. We'd done a couple of duets at church, and we made great harmony together. But there just wasn't the passionate spark between me and Foster that there'd been with Branson. I tried forcing myself to like him, but it wasn't working.

When Bo's car went over that cliff last night, I realized that I wanted to be Branson's girlfriend. I even blurted out that I loved him. Foster heard, and decided to break up with me. He wished me well, but I knew his heart was broken. He thought he was a better fit for me than Branson. I hoped to prove him wrong.

I stared into Branson's deep blue eyes. "I don't have a boyfriend anymore."

"Really?" he asked, a hopeful expression brightening his scratched-up face.

I nodded. "We broke up this morning."

"A beautiful girl like you should always have a boyfriend. Laurel, I know I messed up. I hurt you bad. I made a huge mistake with Brittany. That makes me feel worse than not getting that football scholarship to the University of Georgia."

"Branson, don't rule that out," I said, not ready to discuss the other topics he'd brought up.

Branson Price was the all-star quarterback of our school. When he hurt himself midseason, all the major-league schools stopped trying to recruit him.

"My one shot to walk on as a freshman went out the window when I busted my throwing arm," he groaned.

I kissed his forehead. "Don't talk like that. You have to pray and believe that everything will be all right. Have faith."

He squeezed my hand. "See, that's why I need you in my life. With you I can start all over again. Laurel, I love you. Be my girlfriend again."

I didn't get a chance to answer him because the door swung open and a redheaded nurse entered. "I see you're awake. How are you feeling?"

While Branson assured her he was doing fine, the nurse checked and recorded his vital signs.

"I'll be back to check up on you again before my shift ends."

Branson smiled at her as she walked away.

"Don't get any ideas," I teased him. "She had on a wedding ring."

"Oh, Laurel, it's nothing like that."

"And what *is* it like?"

"Well . . . It's just . . . See, this black nurse came in earlier and she said she was going to give me my checkup. I'm glad a new one came on the schedule before she could get back to me."

"Why?" I asked.

He shuddered. "Just thinking about having a black lady touch me creeps me out, you know?"

I stared at him, appalled that he would say such a thing. "Black women have taken care of white people for years."

"I know, but this isn't the slavery days."

"I'm sure the blacks are more happy about that than you are," I said sarcastically.

"Look, I'm not prejudiced or anything. I have lots of black friends. You know that."

There were some black players on the football team. Jackson Reid, for instance, was one of Branson's best friends. That made me wonder where he was getting all this attitude from.

"Hey, you still haven't answered my question," he asked, pulling me onto the bed beside him. "Will you be my girlfriend?"

I looked into his precious face and softly answered, "Yes."

The next day, Monday, I had to go to school. After that horrible prom, I dreaded the first day back. I even skipped my before-school gymastics practice at Rockdale County Gym and let Brittany drive me to school.

The attitude in the car was somber. Brittany had lost her usual perky demeanor. At school, all the students walked around like zombies. Just like they had last March, after we had that school shooting. My youngest brother, Luke, got shot that day, and so did Faigyn, Foster's younger sister. They were just freshmen, and their lives could have ended. Thank the Lord, both of them were all right.

Our principal, Dr. Wood, called a special assembly first thing. "I know you're all grieving about Saturday's tragedy," she began.

I spotted Foster across the room. His eyes were locked on me until he saw me looking at him. Then he quickly turned away.

Yesterday at church, when he told me it wasn't working out between us because I wasn't committed enough to our relationship, he'd said it was no big deal and that he would be fine without me. But today his eyes revealed a loneliness that wasn't there before. He was hurting.

I saw my girlfriend Robyn walk up to him. He pointed over to me, and she circled around the gym toward me.

Robyn Williams was an African American girl with caramel skin, a cute fluffy haircut, and a lot of backbone. I knew she would stand by me no matter what.

"Hey, girl," Robyn said, taking the seat beside me.

"Shh!" The teacher at the end of our row glared at us.

Robyn rolled her eyes. "She wouldn't give me all that drama if I was a white girl," she said under her breath.

Now, what was that supposed to mean? Did she really feel that way? I was sure that if I'd talked while the principal was speaking, the teacher would have hollered at me too. I was tempted to try it, but didn't want to embarrass myself. So I pretended I didn't hear Robyn's comment.

"Hey, I heard you and Foster broke up," Robyn whispered. "Don't keep all the juice to yourself. What's going on?"

Her slang often made me smile. Not that I longed to imitate it, but she had a neat way of expressing herself. She didn't talk that way all the time. She spoke in proper sentences more often than I did.

"I'll tell you later," I whispered back. "I don't want to get in trouble."

"Girl, forget about that teacher." Robyn's dismissive gesture almost made me laugh.

"That's what I like about you," I said. "You're different."

She shot me an angry glare. "What do you mean, different?"

The teacher leered at us.

"You know," I mouthed. "Different."

"No, Laurel, I don't know," Robyn responded defensively. "Why don't you explain it to me?"

I sighed, wondering what had gotten into her. "I just meant you're not a regular black girl. You wear cool clothes, you live in a nice house, your mom's an author. You don't have gold teeth or tattoos, and you don't live in the projects."

"You know, not every black person is poor."

"I realize that." I glanced at the teacher in our row. This time she looked too engrossed in the principal's speech to notice us. Desperately wanting to change the subject, I asked, "So, you want to hear about me and Foster?"

Her eyes flashed at me. "No, I don't," she snapped. "Foster is the best guy you've ever had. You shouldn't let Branson's little accident convince you to get back together with that jerk. But you know what? I don't even care."

Before I could say anything in response, my friend Meagan Munson, who was sitting on the other side of me, elbowed me. "Listen," she hissed.

I looked up at the principal.

"This has been a difficult year for all of us, but Salem High is still going strong," she was saying. "The sorrowful times we have experienced have made you all stronger. School will be dismissed early today, and all after-school sports practices are cancelled. But I know you will all come back tomorrow with a new attitude, prepared to make the rest of this school year the best it can be."

Normally, I would have been thrilled at the thought of getting out of school early. But I had a very important gymnastics meet coming up and I had been counting on practicing that day. Yet I realized sometimes people have to put their plans on hold when tragedy strikes.

As we all cleared out, I wanted to find Foster and talk to him. But when I looked around the gymnasium, I couldn't find him anywhere.

When I got home that afternoon, my middle brother, Lance, was on the phone, yelling like crazy. The next minute he slammed down the receiver.

"What's wrong with you?" I asked.

"I need to get out of this house," he grumbled, raking his fingers through his short blond hair. "Can you take me for a drive?"

"Sure," I said with a shrug, wondering what his problem was.

As we climbed into the van, Lance said, "Don't just take a short trip."

I pulled out of the garage and headed down the street.

Lance was the quarterback on the sophomore team. He was athletic and popular. He'd had a problem with alcohol, but he conquered that after a binge at Christmas sent him to the hospital and a New Year's Eve party made him pass out. So I didn't know what could be bothering him now. Then I got an idea. Was he still gambling? He'd won and lost quite a bit of money during the first few months of the year, mostly betting on basketball and football games.

"You're gambling again, aren't you?" I asked, my nervous foot pressing harder on the accelerator. "Is someone after you?"

Before he could answer, a police car pulled up behind me, its lights flashing. I was in deep trouble.

I pulled over and looked into the rear view mirror. A

cop in his mid-fifties with a pot belly and freckles sauntered up to my window and asked for my license and registration.

"Shadrach, eh?" he said, examining my paperwork. "The only Shadrach I know is the reverend at Kensington Community Church."

"That's our dad," Lance spoke up. "I just got released from the hospital and my sister—"

"You don't have to explain. I was gonna let you go when I saw y'all were white kids. Often as not, them crazy black troublemakers think the rules don't apply to them. Since y'all are good kids, I'm not gonna rain on your day. You just take it easy, now, ya hear?" The officer handed me back my license and registration, then moseyed on back to his squad car.

"Isn't that sad?" I said to Lance as we pulled back onto the road.

"Sad? It's great! You didn't get a ticket."

"Yeah, but if we were black he would have given us one."

"Well, we're not black, so who cares?"

I ignored his comment and kept driving. But my thoughts raced on. Why was everything around me so black and white all of a sudden? It was starting to bother me. I was going to have to pray about it because I didn't have any answers, and I definitely needed some.

The following day, everybody's spirits had picked up a little. Students acted friendlier to one another. Things were definitely not normal, but they were better.

"Why are you so nervous?" Meagan asked as we stood together in the lunch line. My shy, redheaded friend was cute and sweet, but she could be a little dense sometimes.

"Duh! Tonight is the most important gymnastics meet of our school history. If we win this one, we go on to the regional championships. I've been talking about this for weeks."

"Oh, sure, yeah. I remember."

"I don't know if I'm ready," I confessed. "I've been practicing like crazy, but I'm still having trouble on some of the routines. I really wish we could have practiced yesterday."

"You'll be fine. You're great. How's Branson?"

I sighed. Meagan wasn't athletic, so she couldn't really understand how important this was to me. I decided there was no point in trying to explain. "He's supposed to be getting out of the hospital today."

"That's great. You know, I didn't think you and Branson would ever get back together."

Brittany cut in line behind us. "What are you saying, Meagan? That after I messed him up she'd never want him back?"

"It doesn't matter what went on between you and Branson," I told her. "What's important is that we're back together now, and I hope it lasts forever this time."

When Brittany didn't say anything Meagan spoke up. "If he's who you really want, I hope it works out."

When we sat at our table, I was still kind of mad at Brittany. She just didn't get the concept of true friendship.

"I'm getting some of the other cheerleaders to go to your meet tomorrow," Brittany said.

"You are?" Meagan asked, swallowing a bite of meat loaf.

"Yeah. Everyone knows the great Laurel Shadrach might be going to the Olympics someday and we all want to be there to see her in action." Brittany winked at me. "Branson's coming too. I invited him."

"Brittany, you don't need to call my boyfriend for me," I said. "I have a tongue, I can speak for myself."

"Whatever."

I got up. "You should have at least told me first. I might be a little nervous with Branson at the meet." I threw my lunch in the trash and left the cafeteria. I couldn't eat. I was way too anxious. Something about Branson and Brittany bothered me. Was he coming because he wanted to support me, or because he knew Brittany would be there?

I would never be able to concentrate on the meet with all this confusion going on in my head. I had to pray and give it all to God. I went into the bathroom and prayed until I felt better. It worked wonders. I felt as if a load had been lifted from my shoulders.

I proceeded to the gymnasium, arriving an hour before the meet to practice. As I approached the balance beams, Branson walked up to me and pulled me close to him.

"Branson, you should be at home resting."

"I wanted to support you," he said. Then he kissed me and slid his tongue down my throat.

I wanted to push him away, but I didn't want to make him fall over. "Not here."

"Why not? Because your old boyfriend is looking?"

I didn't know what he was talking about until I turned around and saw Foster standing by the bleachers staring at us. I wasn't sure how to respond so I walked away from both of them.

As I passed Foster he said, "I just came to wish you good luck."

So much for my extra practice. I stormed into the locker room and prayed there until the other gymnasts started showing up.

It was a really close meet. We were coming in second until my event on the balance beam. I had to get at least a 9.98 for our team to win. I closed my eyes, shot up a quick prayer, and did my thing. My body moved effortlessly and I received a perfect ten!

All the girls on both teams ran to the center of the floor and hugged me. Coach Turner picked me up and swung me around so vigorously I nearly kicked a couple of my teammates. But they didn't seem to care. We were going to the regional championships. What a joy it was beating the odds!

messing
things up

Why is *Foster coming over here?* I wondered as I headed toward the locker room after winning the meet.

He smiled at me from across the gym like he wanted to say something. I had no clue where Branson was, but I knew he had to be somewhere in the crowd. Yet I couldn't just walk away. That would be rude. So I prepared myself for Foster's encounter.

Boy, did my smile crack when he walked straight past me and approached Shaney, the sophomore gymnast on our team who had a thing for him. She pulled her short blond hair behind her petite little ears and cooed at him in her babyish voice.

I turned away from them, trying to stop blushing. I stood there for ages, waiting for Branson to come and congratulate me. Coach Milligent and Assistant Coach Weslyn, who had been practicing with me at the Rockdale County Gym for four years, spent several minutes telling me how proud they were of me. Kirsten Wells, Amanda Carson, and Janet Greer, three of the gymnasts from the Rockdale team, gave me big hugs. But Branson never showed up.

My parents came over and suggested we all go out to celebrate. I told them I'd rather hang out with my friends. This was, after all, my senior year, and I wanted to spend time with them while I could.

Just then Brittany and Meagan came up to us. "Hi, Mrs. Shadrach," they greeted in unison.

"Hey, girls," Mom said. "So, what are you planning for tonight?"

"To take the superstar out to celebrate," Brittany said. "Don't worry, we'll be careful."

My parents walked off with a chuckle, and I started searching the crowd again.

"Branson left," Brittany stated.

"You don't have to say it for the whole gym to hear," I said as I noticed Foster looking at me. Shaney was still babbling at him, but I figured he might hear my friends talking to me about Branson. "Maybe I should go find him."

Brittany laid a hand on my arm. "He's fine. He was tired and asked me to tell you congratulations." She pulled me toward the door. "Now, come on. I've got the perfect plans for tonight."

"Wait. I've got to change clothes first."

The two of them headed out the gym doors, and I started for the locker room. On the way a local reporter stopped me.

"Laurel Shadrach, how did you do it?" he asked, sticking a microphone in my face.

"It wasn't me," I said. "It was all God. I couldn't have done it without Him."

I beamed with pride as I strolled to the locker room and changed into street clothes. I was definitely growing as a Christian if I was able to credit everything I did to the Lord.

My thoughts were interrupted by Shaney, the sophomore girl who had just been talking with Foster. "You are so full of yourself, Laurel," she said, her manicured hand on her slender hip. "You think you won the whole thing, don't you? Well, your skills aren't that great. That's why your ex-boyfriend wants me now."

I really wanted to tell her that she certainly didn't contribute anything to the team, but I decided to just ignore her. I started to walk away, but she flung herself at me like a rabid dog. The other gymnasts held her back. I didn't think that was necessary, because there was nothing that puny chick could have done to me anyway.

My friend Robyn burst into the locker room. "What's going on in here?"

"I don't know," I said with a sneer. "This little girl was trying to attack me. I don't know what her problem is."

"Want me to handle her?" Robyn asked, pushing up her sleeves.

"No, I'm fine. She'll settle down in a little while." I took Robyn's arm and we walked out of the locker room, ignoring the little sophomore's taunts.

"I am so proud of you, girl," Robyn said as we crossed the empty gym. She started talking about the plans she'd made for us, and I couldn't break in to tell her about my other friends' plans. When we opened the gym door, I saw Brittany, Meagan, and Kirsten standing in the parking lot.

"It's about time," Brittany said, coming up and grabbing my arm.

"Wait a second, Britt." I turned to Robyn. "I'm afraid I already made plans for tonight. You're welcome to join us."

Robyn stood there for a moment, looking sad and rejected. "That's OK," she finally said. "You guys go have fun." Robyn took off as Brittany pulled me away.

"Britt, you didn't even try to help me convince her."

"She said she didn't want to go," Brittany said. "It didn't seem right to force her. She wouldn't have fit in anyway."

"What does that mean?"

"Laurel, she's black. She doesn't understand us. I just want to have fun and hang out with my friends and . . . well, she's not one of them." Brittany led me toward Meagan and Kirsten, who were still waiting by the car.

I felt terrible. Why couldn't we all hang out together?

"Where are we going?" I asked as Brittany drove down the street, Meagan and Kirsten in the backseat.

"Branson arranged a party for you at Jackson's house," Brittany said.

"On a school night?" I asked.

Brittany rolled her eyes. "Yes," she confirmed in a snotty tone. "To celebrate your great victory."

"Brittany, what's up with you? Why are you being so negative?"

"I'm jealous, OK? Are you happy now?"

I couldn't believe my ears. Brittany's long blond hair, clear blue eyes, and knockout figure made her the kind of girl most other girls would give anything to look like. She lived with her father, who was a doctor. Brittany's brother Gabriel was off at the University of South Carolina, so their father spoiled his daughter like she was an only child. Brittany was a cheerleader, had done some modeling, and had even won beauty pageants.

"How could you be jealous of me?" I asked.

"You were the hero today," she admitted. "I never get to be the hero." She sniffed. "And a party is being planned for you. Your parents are still together but my folks are divorced. My dad is getting ready to date again, and I don't want to have to fight with some other woman for his attention." She lowered her voice. "And besides, you don't have HIV."

Brittany started crying. I did too. Sure, we had our differences, but I hated that she had so much heartache in her life.

"I'm trying not to feel angry every time good things hap-

24

pen for you," Brittany said, wiping her damp cheek as she pulled into Jackson's driveway.

"I'm sorry," I said. "Are you going to be OK?"

"I'm fine. Let's go into this party and liven things up."

I got out of the car and watched Brittany take off into the house. Dozens of cars lined the street on both sides. I wondered what kind of party this was going to be.

Kirsten came up to me and whispered, "Brittany has HIV?"

I hesitated. "Yeah."

"Serves her right for stealing your boyfriend. That's the type of thing girls like her deserve. I can't wait till I tell my neighbor, Chevy Danson. He used to have a huge crush on her, remember?"

"Kirsten, don't spread that around. Brittany's my friend and I care about her."

"Hey, no problem. I'll keep it a secret if you want me to," she promised.

I sighed in relief, glad that she thought enough of our friendship to keep quiet about my best friend's problem.

"I'm really going to miss you," I said, putting my arm around her. Kirsten's dad had accepted a big job promotion that required her family to move to New York. They were staying in Georgia until after graduation, but planned to leave right after that.

"I'm gonna miss you too," she said. "If it wasn't for you, I'd probably still be bulimic and a junkie. You've really made a difference in my life."

"God made the difference," I said, wanting to give credit to the right source. "Don't ever forget that."

"I won't," she promised.

As we walked into the house, it occurred to me that Jackson Reid was having a party and Robyn, his girlfriend, wasn't welcome. Brittany had said she wouldn't fit in. But there were plenty of other black people around—even some people Robyn hung out with at school.

I looked for Brittany, but all I found was a bunch of

football players around a keg of beer. I was happy that Branson and Brittany were nowhere near it. Then again, I thought, where were they?

I decided to check upstairs. Sure enough, the two of them were talking in one of the bedrooms . . . alone.

"What's going on?" I asked.

They both looked up with guilty expressions. "It's not what you think," Brittany assured me. "I had to tell Branson I was sorry for maybe giving him a disease."

"I still have one more test," Branson said. "I'm not out of the woods yet."

I decided to drop it. Obviously HIV was still weighing heavily on his mind, and if he needed to talk about it he should.

"Did you want something?" Brittany asked.

Remembering the reason I'd gone looking for her in the first place, I sat on the bed beside her. "I was just wondering why Robyn couldn't come to this party. I mean, she *is* Jackson's girlfriend."

Brittany shrugged. "He didn't want her to come. He asked me not to tell her about the party. Talk to him about it."

I was boiling. This made no sense. I stormed downstairs and found Jackson in the kitchen. I wondered where his foster parents were, knowing that if they were around, Jackson wouldn't be having this kind of party.

As soon as he saw me, he pinned me to the wall. His breath reeked of alcohol. "You know, you look good for a white girl. I never even noticed until I saw you in that leotard today. Man, you've got a nice body." I tried to squirm out of his hold, but he was too strong for me. He licked my ear. "Maybe when you get tired of Branson you can give me a try."

Branson suddenly showed up and shoved Jackson across the kitchen. "What are you doing with my girl?" he yelled.

26

"Hey, man, I was just playin'," Jackson said, leaning against a counter.

"Well, back off, all right?"

"Sure," Jackson said. "It's cool."

They smacked hands and Jackson left. Branson pulled me toward him and kissed me passionately. Boy, did I love him.

The next morning I woke up to the wonderful smells of bacon and blueberry pancakes. I couldn't believe Mom had made me a special breakfast on a school day.

"You got an important call last night," my mom said when I came downstairs.

Liam, my oldest brother, was smiling from ear to ear. "Somebody's going to college."

"What are you talking about?" I asked, tossing a few slices of bacon onto a plate.

"Coach Burrows called," Mom said.

I almost dropped my dish. "From UGA?"

"Yes," Dad said. "She said she's going to the regional championships on Saturday, and she's looking forward to watching you compete. If she likes what she sees, she has the authority to offer you a scholarship."

My heart was racing. Going to the University of Georgia had been my dream since I moved to Conyers from Conway, Arkansas, four years ago. I didn't know whether to laugh or cry or jump up and down like a little kid.

"I can't wait to tell Coach Turner and Coach Milligent!" I gobbled down a couple of pancakes and washed them down with a full glass of orange juice, my heart pounding.

After school, I stopped by Mrs. Turner's office and gave her the great news. Then I flew to Rockdale Gym for my after-school practice.

"You're five minutes late, Ms. Shadrach," Coach Milligent said when I burst through the doors. "An Olympic gymnast always has her priorities in order."

"Sorry, Coach," I said, catching my breath.

I kept the news about UGA to myself until after I showed my coach what I could do. After a great practice I told him all about it, and he was thrilled for me. Then I called Branson.

"Hey," he said right away, "you got any plans for tonight?"

"Yeah, I've got to study for finals."

"But I want to take you out."

"Branson, I can't. I've got to get good grades so I don't jeopardize my chances of getting into UGA."

"Fine," Branson grumbled and hung up on me. I didn't even have a chance to tell him my great news.

As I was trying to forget about my boyfriend and concentrate on studying, my Sunday school teacher, Mrs. Meaks, called to ask me if I was planning to come to the new discipleship group at her house the next day.

"I don't know," I told her. "I've been pretty busy lately. Besides a ton of year-end homework, I've got gymnastics practice at Rockdale before school on Mondays and Wednesdays, and on Tuesdays and Thursdays after school, and every Saturday from nine to twelve. Not to mention the practices for the school team every Monday and Wednesday after school."

"Sounds like a pretty heavy schedule," Mrs. Meaks said.

"It is," I agreed. "But I'll never make the Olympic team if I don't put in the practice time."

"Just don't get too busy for God, Laurel," she said. "That's never a wise decision."

"Yeah, I know," I mumbled.

"We'll be meeting every Thursday at six, and if you decide you want to come you'll be more than welcome. If your practice runs past six, I won't mind if you're late. That would be better than not coming at all."

"I'll try," I said, not really planning to.

The next day after school, I went to the Rockdale County

Gym for my usual practice. Unfortunately, I couldn't concentrate because of everything that was going on in my life.

As I completed one of the more difficult routines on the parallel bars, I landed wrong on my left ankle . . . the same one I'd sprained the past fall. Shooting pains raked through my body.

I started screaming and crying. How could this happen? There went my dreams. There went my future. I had ruined my life. Why was I always so successful at messing things up?

deciding
on georgia

m y ankle, my ankle!" I screamed, tears welling up in my
eyes.

Coach Milligent raced me over to me.

"I don't understand," I groaned. "Things were going
great for me. And now this. Why?"

Coach Milligent handed me a glass of water. I chucked it
across the room. The sound of shattering glass brought me
back to reality.

"I'm so sorry." I wept hysterically as he examined my ankle.

I knew Coach Milligent was just as angry as I was. I was
waiting for him to say everything was OK, that it wasn't that
bad of an injury. But he never did. He didn't even fuss at me,
so I knew something was seriously wrong.

"I'll call 911," he said. "And your parents."

When the paramedics showed up, they examined my
swollen ankle. Shooting pain ripped through my leg every
time they touched it.

"Well," one of the paramedics said, "it doesn't look broken. But it is sprained badly. We'll have to take you in for X-rays."

"She's injured that ankle before," Coach Milligent said, shaking his head.

"We can give you some medication for the pain," the other paramedic said.

I nodded, unable to speak. They could give me something for the pain in my body, but who would soothe the pain I felt in my soul?

As if God had heard my prayer, my mom walked in and held me tightly.

"It's over, Mom," I cried. "It's over."

I woke up later that afternoon in my own bed. I wanted it all to be a dream, but the pain in my ankle reminded me it was real. I was so angry. The only thing I had ever wanted was to do well in gymnastics. I didn't understand why God hadn't allowed me to stay injury free.

"You could have stopped it, You know," I said, talking to Him as if He were sitting right on the edge of my bed. "How could You do this to me? How could You crush my dreams like this?"

Just then my dad walked in. "How are you doing, honey?" He sat on my bed where I had imagined God had been.

"I'll be OK. I'm just disappointed." For some reason, I couldn't lash out at my dad, the good reverend.

"I'm proud of you, Laurel. I know how much you wanted to compete in the championships next weekend, especially with Coach Burrows planning to be there. But don't worry. It's all going to work out."

"You're right, Dad," I said, not believing a word of it.

My dad stood and kissed my forehead. As he left the room, Brittany and Meagan swooped in.

"Hey, Laurel, cheer up," Brittany said. "We're here!"

"So, guess you guys heard, huh?" I said.

"Yeah," Meagan said. "Are you OK?"

"It's just stupid gymnastics. I don't care."

"I told you she wasn't thinking about that dumb old sport," Brittany said. "Well, since you're doing fine, let's give you a facial. Meagan, run out and find me some towels and hot water."

I really wasn't into having one of Brittany's facials. The last time she gave me one she left some of the green spinach mask on my face and no one told me. The edges of my face were tight and dry for the next couple of days. She was more used to getting facials than giving them. Being her guinea pig wasn't much fun anytime, and I sure wasn't in the mood right then.

When Meagan left to get the things needed for Brittany's experiment, my best friend hopped onto the bed and leaned in closely. "OK, give me all the dirt."

"What are you talking about?"

"Branson told me about Jackson. What's going on with you and him?"

"Nothing's going on. Jackson is Robyn's man."

"Oh, yeah?" Brittany said. "Well, he's definitely cheating on her. If he'd put the moves on you right under Branson's nose, you know he's got to be doing it with other girls."

When Meagan returned, she and Brittany proceeded with my pampering session, and I had to admit it did cheer me up a little. When they left, I thought about telling God how thankful I was for my two good friends. But I was still angry with Him, so I said nothing.

All night I felt devastated, unable to think of anything besides my injury. When the phone rang, I decided to let one of my brothers get it. Minutes later Luke ran in and told me that my boyfriend was on the phone.

I picked up the receiver. "Hi, Branson."

"I heard the bad news," he said.

"I'm so upset. Now I won't be able to play in the regional championship this weekend. And Coach Burrows from UGA was coming to see me compete. I won't get another chance for a scholarship. Branson, what am I going to do? The doctor said this is a minor sprain, so I won't need a cast. But my ankle won't really heal for another six to eight weeks."

"I understand how you feel. Remember how angry I was last fall when I lost the UGA scholarship? Then I had to watch Jackson sign an offer for Georgia. I want to tell you something, though, Laurel. You've got to stay positive. This is not the end of the world."

"Yeah, I know," I mumbled.

"I'm thinking of walking on for football."

"Walking on?" I asked. "What's that?"

"The football coach holds a certain number of spots for players who have potential, but weren't able to get scholarships. If one of the main players gets hurt, there's a chance I could take his spot, and then I could show the coach what I'm made of."

I felt a glimmer of hope. Maybe I could "walk on" to the gymnastics team.

"I'm going up to Georgia tomorrow to talk to the football coach," he said. "You can go with me, if you want, and talk to Coach Burrows. We could leave right after school tomorrow. It's only a forty-minute drive."

I really liked having Branson back in my life. He was so encouraging. And he understood me, which made it really easy to be myself with him. I told him I'd love to go to UGA with him.

"Are you going to school tomorrow?" he asked.

"I don't know. I feel pretty out of it."

"Why don't you get some sleep so I won't have to miss that beautiful face."

I laughed. "Hey, how is Bo doing?" I asked, curious

about his friend who'd been driving when they got in that horrible car accident on prom night.

"He's out of the coma, but his doctors say he'll probably never walk again."

My heart sank. "I'm going to have to pray for him." I knew God could choose to heal Bo. I just didn't know if He would. Bo had always been antagonistic about God. I'd tried a few times to talk to him about the Lord, but he always shut me down right away, telling me in no uncertain terms that he wanted nothing to do with anything "religious."

"Branson, about the other night, when I found you and Brittany upstairs at Jackson's party. I'm sorry for not trusting you."

"Yeah, well, you had reason to have your guard up."

"But if we're going to start over, I need to really trust you."

"Do you trust me now?"

"Yeah, I do. And I love you."

We laughed and joked and he sent me a kiss over the phone. My leg didn't hurt so much and I was able to get some sleep.

But when morning came I didn't feel up to going to school. My foot was so swollen I couldn't even stand. I did have a better attitude, though. Mom made me a ham and cheddar omelet, which she brought up to my room. It tasted great. But that got me thinking about how much I would miss my mother when I went off to college.

"What's wrong?" Mom asked when she came in to pick up my breakfast tray.

"I'm gonna miss you."

She sat in the chair beside my bed. "Laurel, if I could keep you and your brothers young forever, I would. But you've become a wonderful young lady, and I'm sure you'll make wise decisions when you're on your own." She took my hand. "I know you're upset about your sprained ankle. But I hope you don't lose faith in yourself or in God. Sometimes we don't get what we want, but that just means God has another plan."

I told my mom how angry I was with God for allowing this to happen to me.

She smiled. "Laurel, did you know that before I married your father, I wanted to write Christian novels?"

"Really? That's what Robyn's mom does. What happened?"

"I had kids. So I gave up that dream for motherhood. But I've never regretted it for a minute. I love you and your brothers so much. And who knows? Maybe, after you're all grown up, I can publish a book after all."

I hugged my mother tightly. "Thanks," I said.

———————————

"I can't believe your parents hired a driver to take us to Athens," I said to Branson as we rode to UGA in a luxurious black limousine.

"My dad doesn't want me driving yet," Branson said. "Too soon after the accident. Besides, he didn't figure you and your crutches would fit very well in the Camaro."

Branson held my hand all the way to the campus. We both felt really nervous.

The driver stopped at the gymnastics building first. "You ready?" Branson asked.

"Oh, yeah," I said, stepping gingerly on my bandaged foot. "I'm gonna convince that lady that I'm ready to be on the team."

"That's my girl," Branson said, grinning proudly at me before the driver took off for the football stadium.

I hobbled to the gym using the same crutches I'd used the first time I sprained my ankle. When I got there I found the coach's door closed. I knocked gently. The door opened and a curly-haired brunette said, "Hello. I'm Coach Burrows. What can I do for you?"

"I'm Laurel Shadrach."

"From Conyers, right? I was supposed to come see you compete tomorrow. But from the looks of those bandages, you won't be there."

She offered me a seat and brought me a Sprite. As I looked into her brown eyes, I felt really good about deciding on Georgia.

f o u r

smiling
deep within

a big smile plastered itself across my face. In spite of my nervousness, I'd presented my case clearly, expressing my desires and explaining my abilities well. The coach was about to tell me if I would be going to this school. Though I couldn't show her my ability, I was sure she wouldn't want to lose someone with my enthusiasm and talent. I was going to be a Georgia Bulldog!

"Laurel," Coach Burrows said, "you're obviously a great athlete, and we'd really like to have you here at Georgia. Unfortunately, my hands are tied. I've only got one scholarship left, and this is the second time you've injured that ankle within the last year. You represent everything I want my gymnasts to be. But I can't give scholarships based on my heart."

My eyes filled with tears.

She came from around her desk and sat beside me. "I know how badly you want this. Maybe we can figure out a solution that'll work for both of us."

I couldn't even look at her. I knew I deserved a break. I had competed in regional and national competitions since I was ten. I was twenty-third in the country, and everyone predicted I'd be going to the Olympics in four years.

"Laurel, I do have one walk-on spot. If you can pay for college the first year, and prove yourself during that time, then you might get a scholarship for the rest of the years you're here."

That was the news I'd wanted to hear. But then it hit me. How in the world could I pay for a full year's tuition at UGA?

"Look, you're an outstanding athlete," Coach Burrows said. "I would hate to lose you. But if you don't want to wait for UGA, I'm sure Florida State University or Alabama would give you a shot. On the other hand, if you want to be on the best team on the east coast, I suggest you take the walk-on spot. If you're as good as you seem to be, the scholarship could be yours at the end of the first semester."

"Thanks," I whispered.

"Why don't you go home and talk it over with your parents. Call me when you've made a decision."

The tears in my eyes flowed onto my cheeks. Coach Burrows handed me a box of tissues. I gave her a half smile. She really was a nice person. I'd talked to coaches from other schools and they didn't seem to care about their players as people.

I wondered if my parents would have enough money to send me to school even for a semester. Most of Dad's income was tied up in church ministries and missions.

When I left the gym, I saw the limo parked across the street. The driver got out right away and helped me into the backseat, placing my crutches on the ample floor space. As we drove to the stadium to pick up Branson, I prayed. *Lord, You know my heart so You know I'm not angry. However, I am disappointed. I need You to help me find a way to get to Georgia.*

Even as I came to Him asking for finances, I decided to give the whole situation to Him. *I'm not going to let this burden me,* I told the Lord. *I know You'll straighten everything out.*

A tapping sound interrupted my prayer. Branson pressed his face against the window. Things must have gone well for him because he was acting silly. When he got in the car he started bouncing with joy.

As we headed back toward Conyers, Branson told me the football coach was excited that he was thinking of walking on. He said he was sure Branson could get a scholarship. The coach showed him around the campus and introduced him to the football staff.

"I'm going to Georgia, Laurel. I'm gonna make the team."

Branson didn't ask me how my meeting went. There was a time when I would have thought that was selfish, but I was glad for him and I didn't want to bring him down with my bad news.

When we stopped to pick up some fast food, Branson said, "I'm sorry. I've been rambling on and on about my talk with the coach. How did yours go?"

"Coach Burrows basically told me the same thing," I said, munching on a french fry. "She's giving me the chance to walk on too."

"That's great!" He kissed me on the cheek, then wiped a spot of ketchup off my chin with his napkin. "We're both going to Georgia, Laurel."

I smiled, even though I wasn't totally confident. Still, I convinced myself to get excited. I refused to go to a second-rate college. Branson and I were going to work hard for our dreams. We were going to Georgia, and I was sure we'd both make an impact on our teams.

The winding two-lane road that led to my house was almost impossible to see at night without the brights on. When the limo swerved, almost hitting a tree, the driver opened the glass divider and apologized. "A black SUV just flew past me," he explained.

When we were almost to my house, the driver hit his

brakes and pulled over. "There's someone in the road," he said. The driver shot out of the car. Branson opened his door.

"Please don't go," I said, not wanting to be left alone in the car. "Stay here with me."

"I need to help," he said, getting out of the car.

Branson wasn't out there a minute before he yelled back to me. I grabbed my crutches and hobbled out of the car. I gasped when I saw my brother, Lance, lying in the street. He'd been beaten to a bloody pulp.

"Oh, my gosh! What happened?"

"You said Lance owes a lot of money to some pretty nasty people," Branson said as he picked my brother up off the road. "Maybe he couldn't pay them and they gave him a warning."

When Branson laid my brother down in the back of the limo, Lance screamed out in pain. I lifted his shirt and saw blue, black, and purple bruises all over his chest.

"Now I know why that SUV drove by so fast," the limo driver said, getting back in.

When we reached my house, I was relieved to see my parents' cars in the driveway. I limped inside and hollered for my mom and dad.

"Laurel, what's wrong?" Mom asked, flying down the stairs.

"It's Lance," I said as Branson helped my brother into the house.

"Dave!" Mom called out. "Liam!"

As the limo driver called for an ambulance, Branson and I told my family what we knew.

"I'm sorry, Mom," I wailed as I cried in her arms.

"Sorry about what?"

"Lance has been gambling. He owes some people money, but he asked me not to tell you and Dad. He promised me he was going to stop. This is all my fault."

"No, Laurel, it's not. But this does shed some light on things." My mother looked at my dad. "What did we do wrong?"

My father put his arms around her, but she jerked away.

Lord, help my family, I prayed.

After the ambulance took Lance to the hospital, with my parents following in the van, the limo driver told Branson he needed to get him back home.

"Are you going to be OK?" Branson asked me.

"I'll be fine."

"I'll call you when I get home," he promised before he left.

I looked at Liam, who had a worried expression on his face. I reached over and punched my oldest brother in the arm. "God's got this. He's going to work everything out."

"Yeah," he said. "I know. Everything's going to be fine."

———————

The next day was the regional championships. I'd planned to go to cheer on my team, even though I couldn't compete. Instead I spent the day at the hospital with Lance and my parents. While he was sleeping, I told Mom and Dad about my meeting with Coach Burrows.

"Is there any way we could afford at least the first semester's tuition at UGA?"

My dad shook his head. "I'm sorry, honey. But we haven't been able to save up enough money for you or your brothers to go to an expensive college."

"I can get a job," I suggested.

"It'll be mighty difficult for you to get good grades in college and impress the coach with your gymnastics abilities if you're also working, even part-time," Mom said.

"And you couldn't earn enough to cover all the costs of tuition and books and everything else," Dad added.

"What about the HOPE Scholarship?" I asked. I'd been reading about it in a brochure my guidance counselor gave me, so I was ready to present the facts to my parents. "It covers full tuition, health fees, the student activity fee, and a book allowance for the first two years at any accredited Georgia college."

My dad shook his head. "Laurel, do you know where that money comes from?"

I racked my brain, envisioning the brochure in my mind. I didn't recall reading anything that explained the origin of the scholarship.

"It's lotto money, Laurel," Dad explained. "It would go against my principles to utilize something that was funded that way. I know too many people whose lives have been ruined by compulsive gambling. And now it looks like Lance is another victim of that particular sin."

I took a deep breath. I'd been sure the HOPE Scholarship was heaven-sent to accomplish my dreams. I'd never imagined that my parents would find a problem with it.

"Maybe it's not God's will for you to go to UGA after all," Mom suggested.

Tears stung my eyes. "I can't go to a community college that doesn't even have a gymnastics team," I cried. But I couldn't see any other way.

"Dang it, black guys make me sick," Liam complained out of the blue as we sat in his room with Luke the next day. I had come in to ask my brothers when they wanted to give Mom her Mother's Day gift, but the discussion took a sudden, nasty turn.

"What do you mean?" Luke asked.

"Lance told me the whole story. Some loan sharks in Decatur didn't want to give him a chance to pay back the money he borrowed, so they beat him up."

"I'm sure color had nothing to do with it," I said, tired of all the racial bashing I'd been hearing lately.

"I don't know. The barbaric way they beat him up, it's like they're animals."

"Listen to yourself," I said. "You sound so ignorant."

"I'm just mad, OK?" He punched his fist against the wall.

"So, what are you gonna do?" Luke asked, his brown eyes gleaming. "Get a gun and shoot the guy?"

"Don't even joke about that," I cried.

"Hey, you saw what they did to Lance," Liam said.

"Revenge is never a good solution," I said, looking hard at both of them.

"How much does he owe?" Luke asked. "Maybe we could pay the guys off."

"Six thousand dollars," Liam said with a sneer.

My youngest brother whistled. "How could he get himself into that much debt?"

"He probably placed more bets than he could cover," I said.

We all sat in silence, trying to come up with a way to help our brother.

"We could take back the present we got for Mom," Liam suggested hesitantly. "That cost two hundred dollars."

"I'm sure she'd rather have Lance alive and healthy than a fancy new blender," Luke said.

"That wouldn't even make a dent," I said. "What's the point of doing that if there's no way to get the rest of the money?"

"I guess Mom and Dad will have to take some cash out of savings," Liam said. "Good thing you're getting that scholarship."

Before I could correct him, I heard our parents come in the front door. I started to run down to meet them, but stopped halfway down the stairs when I heard them arguing in the kitchen.

"Why are you so mad?" my dad growled, slamming his fist on a cabinet. "All I did was make a decision."

I snuck down a few steps so I could see what was going on better.

"I can't believe you'd commit us to something like this without even discussing it with me." Mom tossed her purse onto the counter with a thud.

"You make decisions without asking me," my dad shot back.

"No, I don't. I take everything to you."

Liam joined me on the stairs and sat on the next step up, his face lined with concern.

My dad opened the refrigerator door and glared at the contents. Then he grabbed a loaf of bread, a jar of mustard, and a package of lunchmeat and smacked them onto the countertop.

"I can't believe you're going to bring someone else into our house," Mom said, watching him make a sandwich. "This is not the time to be ministering to other people. Your family needs you. We're falling apart."

"Just because our kids have a few priorities out of order does not mean we're falling apart," he grumbled, yanking open the silverware drawer. "I care about their well-being, so don't you dare say I put everything above them. That's not true and it's unfair." He pulled a knife out of the drawer and slammed it closed.

"What about Laurel's college?"

My father took a long, slow breath.

"You know how badly she wants to go to UGA. But our money is so tied up in missionaries and building funds and all the other church ministries, there's not enough left to make your own children's dreams come true."

I held my breath. *Come on, Dad,* I begged silently. *Tell her that's not true. Say that you've been setting aside* something *for my education.*

But my father just stood there, spreading mustard on his bread.

"Not only do you invest all your money in the church, all your time is spent there too," Mom went on. "If you paid more attention to your sons, maybe Lance wouldn't have become an alcoholic and a gambler."

Dad's mustard-covered knife stopped in midair. "I can't believe you said that."

Mom's hand flew to her mouth, as if she wished more than anything that she could take back the words that had just escaped from there. "I'm sorry," she said softly. "That was over the line."

Dad looked at Mom with misty eyes. "Laura, I don't know why God is leading me to bring a black guy into our home. But I am absolutely convinced it's the right thing to do."

Shock waves rippled across Liam's face. "I can't believe this," he mumbled as he went back up to his room. I stayed put to see what else I could find out.

"This young man has been living in the dorms at Georgia Tech," Dad said. "I met him when I spoke at a chapel there last fall, and he really touched my heart. He never knew his father, and his mom's on drugs. I've kept in touch with him since then. He's really a great kid." Dad sliced his sandwich in half. "Anyway, they're renovating the dorms this summer, and he has nowhere to go. He has a grandmother in Sly County, but that's a three-hour drive from here. If he stayed with her, he wouldn't be able to work out at the college to prepare for next year's team."

Dad offered Mom the first bite of the sandwich, which she took with a small smile.

"I know I shouldn't have told him he could come without talking it over with you first. And you're right. We've got to figure out what's wrong with our children before we lose them."

"I love you, David Paul Shadrach," Mom said, giving him back the sandwich. "Our children do have some problems, but at least they're still here."

That afternoon, Mom and Dad went to the hospital and picked up Lance. The whole left side of his face was swollen. But the doctors said he would be fine.

In the evening, as we sat around the dining room table eating orange duck, my brothers and I made an extra effort to thank my mom for everything she'd ever done for us.

Mom really appreciated the blender, and she said she couldn't wait to use it to make us all chocolate shakes . . . when we weren't so full from dinner.

No one said anything about bringing in a houseguest. So I kept quiet, too, not wanting to admit that I'd been eavesdropping, and not wanting to spoil the happy mood.

Seeing my parents hugging and kissing was great. Though my family definitely had issues, God was still the head of our house and I felt His presence. That made me feel so good, I was smiling deep within.

welcoming
a stranger

this is crazy," Liam said, getting up from the dinner table the next night and storming out of the room.

Dad's forehead crinkled in anger and Mom looked disappointed. Obviously, they'd hoped their announcement would be met with more support.

"Stay here," I said. "I'll go talk to him." I hobbled up the stairs, getting pretty good at moving around with my crutches.

Liam and I hadn't seen eye to eye on a lot of things lately. A hatred was building up inside my oldest brother that I was having a hard time dealing with. He was normally so calm and cool, with a level head on his shoulders.

Lord, I prayed as I walked down the hall to my brothers' room, *I don't know what to say to him. I don't even understand where all his anger is coming from. Please use me to make things better.*

The moment I stepped into the room, Liam said, "I don't want to talk right now. Just go away."

I turned around. But before I could walk out, my dad came in.

"Liam, it is unacceptable for you to talk to your sister like that. And the way you left the table requires an apology to the whole family. If you have something you'd like to talk about, say so. This childish behavior of yours is no way to get attention."

Liam glared at Dad. "You want to know what's bothering me? I'll tell you. How could you bring a black guy here to live with us? You're trying to be a father to some worthless orphan when you can't even take care of your own son. Is that direct enough?"

Liam brushed past us and stomped downstairs, almost knocking over my crutches. Dad just stood there. I could tell he wanted to spank Liam or shake him or hold him. But he just stood there as if he couldn't move. So I hugged him.

"I love you, Dad. Liam's just angry. I don't know what it's about, but I know it's not really about you."

Dad flopped onto Lance's bed. "So, what's your opinion about bringing someone into our house?"

I paused. "Honestly? I agree with Mom and Liam. Now doesn't seem like the best time. But if God is directing you to do this, then it's going to work out."

My father stood, patted my arm, and strutted downstairs. I had no idea where Liam had gone, but Mom had cooked a delicious meal and I was going to go back and enjoy it.

Later that night we all assembled in the living room. Liam was still pouting, but he was present. Lance looked more bruised than ever. Luke sat in the corner playing with his computer, not paying attention to anyone.

Dad took charge and opened in prayer. "Heavenly Father, right now everyone in this house is feeling different things. But each one of us needs one thing, and that's You. God, I'm thankful that You allowed me to be the head of this household. I recognize the strain that my being a preacher puts on my children. I know sometimes they see me caring for others and they think I don't care as much for them. Lord, I'm coming to You right now, asking You to help me be the father I need to be. Help my wife be the mother You called her to be. Help my children understand my role as a pastor. I ask You to come into our home right now and let all that we say and do be centered around You. In Your precious name we pray. Amen."

Dad opened his eyes. "Guys, I love you all, and I'm sorry. I know I'm not a perfect dad, but I do want to be. I don't know why God told me to bring someone else into this house at this time, but now that the decision has been made I need you guys to support me. I don't want to bring this young man into our home and have him not feel welcome. Derek Maddox is a great guy. He's really making a difference at Georgia Tech, not just with football, but with his testimony."

"He's a football player?" Lance asked, perking up a little.

"Yes," my dad said, "going into his senior year in the fall. Matter of fact, he's their starting linebacker. He's a strong Christian, too, and he's doing very well in the engineering program at Georgia Tech. Most important, he's a firm believer in Jesus Christ."

That pleased Liam, who was a strong Christian, and Luke, who was into engineering. All three of them would have something in common with this guy.

Liam apologized to my parents for being a jerk. We all agreed to support Dad's decision to invite Derek into our house.

———————

"I need to talk to you," Robyn said to me at school a few days later.

My girlfriend and I hadn't spoken for almost two weeks. I'd tried to talk to her, but she kept giving me an attitude, saying things like "Talk to the hand." Though I missed our friendship, I wasn't up for an argument.

"I'm really not in the mood." I started to walk away, but the look on Robyn's face stopped me.

"Laurel," she said, her eyes filled with tears, "I just need to know one thing. Why do you keep using racial slurs?"

I blushed. "What are you talking about?"

"You don't even know you're doing it, do you? I think part of you is prejudiced."

"You're crazy."

"Am I?"

"Look, I've got to get to class, but you're right about one thing. We definitely need to talk. Can we get together after school?"

"Meet you at my car?" she suggested.

"I'll be there," I promised.

As I walked out of my last class I thought about what I would say to Brittany and Meagan. I'd promised to ride home with them. I hadn't done much with them lately because I'd been spending most of my time with Branson.

Brittany walked up to me in the hallway. "I've got great plans for this afternoon."

"I'm sorry, Britt, but I've got to back out."

"This was supposed to be our time," she whined. "You can't hang out with Branson every night."

"It's not Branson. I've got to spend some time with Robyn."

She raised her eyebrows at me. "You're choosing that black chick over me?"

"There's something I need to take care of with her."

Brittany rolled her eyes and stormed away. I sighed and headed for the parking lot..

"So, why do you think I'm a racist?" I asked Robyn as we drove down highway 138 in her black Toyota.

"You're always making little jokes about things I do or say."

"Like what?"

"I don't know. Like using slang terms and stuff."

"Such as?"

Robyn sputtered and stuttered, but didn't come up with an example.

"Look, if you can't tell me what I said, how can you accuse me of being a racist?"

"Are you one?"

"No! I'm not that familiar with black culture, but that's because I'm white. It's like you're getting mad at me because I'm not black."

Robyn drove in silence for a while, then pulled into a beautiful park with a small lake surrounded by trees. She turned toward an area with shaded picnic tables, away from the kiddie playground.

"Other than me," she asked as she turned off the engine, "how many black friends do you have?"

I hesitated for a second, and she jumped on me right away. "Don't even answer that. You only know one other black person. My boyfriend, Jackson Reid. And I know you came on to him at a party."

"Who told you that?"

"He did. Guess that explains why I wasn't invited." She got out of the car, slammed the door, and stomped off across the long grass.

I had a hard time following her on my crutches until she stopped beside a picnic table under a tree in a fairly secluded area of the park.

"Look, Robyn," I said, panting to catch my breath, "the only reason Brittany didn't want you to go to the party was that Jackson told her not to bring you. He's the one who didn't want you there."

She glared at me. "You're just saying that to hurt me."

"Just the opposite," I said as I collapsed onto the cool grass. "I've been avoiding saying it because I didn't want to hurt you. But I don't want to be lied about."

Robyn plopped down on the seat of the picnic table, obviously trying to take in what I had just told her.

"Look," I said, "you told me you weren't going to pursue a relationship with Jackson after he got you pregnant. Then, after you miscarried, you guys got intimately involved again. It's like you didn't learn anything, and that makes me mad. Apparently you were just kidding when you told God you were sorry."

"What makes you so high and mighty?"

"Nothing," I said, pulling my knees up to my chin. "I just think we're on two totally different pages. But it's not a race thing. It's a Christian thing. I have a problem when someone says they're not going to do something anymore and then they just keep sinning. And now you're listening to this jerk telling you I wanted him."

She stared at the ducks on the pond for a few minutes. I pulled out several blades of grass. I figured she was angry with me, but I'd only told her the truth, so I couldn't feel bad about that.

"OK," she finally said. "Maybe I do owe you an apology. Jackson probably was lying to me. I just keep getting this funny feeling that he's cheating on me. Laurel, I think I love him, but I don't want to be stupid. I don't have anyone to talk to about all this."

"What about your mom?" I asked, watching a duck waddle out of the water and head toward us. "She's cool."

Robyn didn't speak for a long time. When I looked at her, I saw tears rolling down her cheeks. "Mom's doctor found a lump in her breast," she choked out.

I quickly stood and joined her on the picnic bench. "Oh, Robyn, I'm so sorry."

"Life is just not fair," she blurted out.

I put my arm around my friend as she sobbed.

She put her head into my shoulder and cried. "Laurel, what if something happens to my mom? What if she dies, like my dad?"

I wrapped my other arm around her and wept with her. I wanted to share her burdens, and help her give them all to

God. I wanted to let her know that He would be there for her to help her through her pain.

I saw a couple walking down the nearby sidewalk, pushing their baby in a stroller and cooing to it. They looked like a cute, happy family. But I didn't think that was the kind of thing Robyn would want to be seeing right then.

When her sobbing subsided a little, I said, "You want to come to my house and have some popcorn?"

She smiled through her pain. "Yeah."

As she drove back, I asked if I could pray for her. I did, and that seemed to make her feel a little better. We were even able to laugh at a kid trying to do skateboarding tricks on a curb.

When Robyn and I walked into the house, she stopped at the doorway to the hall and whispered, "Who is that fine thing coming out of your bathroom?"

I joined her and saw a tall black guy wearing a towel around his waist . . . and nothing else! His short black hair looked damp, and his amazingly chiseled muscles made me gasp.

Apparently he heard me or Robyn or both of us, because he turned around quickly, a shocked expression on his fine-featured face. "Excuse me, ladies," he said as he darted toward the guest room.

"That must be Derek," I said.

"Who's Derek? And where have you been hiding him?" she joked.

"He's our new houseguest. I haven't met him yet."

"Can I live here?" Robyn asked with a grin.

I grabbed her arm and pulled her into the kitchen. "Let's just get some ice-cold lemonade to cool us off!"

The popcorn had just started popping when my mother came in. "Laurel, there's someone I'd like you to meet."

She stepped farther into the room and the hunk from the hallway came in behind her, dressed in a polo shirt and khakis. "Girls, this is Derek Maddox. Derek, this is my daughter, Laurel, and her friend Robyn."

Derek extended a hand to us. "Hello again, ladies." He flashed a big smile filled with perfect white teeth.

"You are so fine," Robyn whispered.

"Pardon me?" he asked.

"I mean, the pleasure's all mine." Robyn giggled.

Derek's smile widened. "Well, I'd better get going. There's a project I want to work on upstairs." He left, and my mom followed him out.

"He can work on my project anytime," Robyn said.

The two of us laughed and screamed and fanned ourselves, then took lots of long drinks of our cold lemonade.

———————

"What are you doing in my room?" Derek was sitting at my desk, with my computer in pieces all over the place.

"I'm sorry. Didn't your dad tell you I was working on your computer?"

"No, he didn't."

"He said your family's computers are all old, and he wanted to buy some new ones. But I told him I could get new programs and parts and fix up the ones you've got."

"Really?"

"Really," he said with a slight grin. He went back to work on my computer, and I sat in the nearby chair. "Your dad also told me you're a gymnast," he said without looking up from his work. "From all the awards around here, I can see you must be pretty talented."

I blushed at the thought that this guy had been in my room, looking at my personal stuff. I did a quick visual check to make sure I hadn't left any underwear lying around.

"I thought I'd be finished with this by the time you came back up," he said. "Sorry. I'll be out of your way in a minute." He pulled something green and rectangular and important-looking out of the inside of my computer.

I felt kind of bad. Here he was trying to do something

nice for me and I was giving him an attitude. "No, I'm sorry," I said. "Please don't rush because of me."

I sat there watching him work. "Did you learn all that stuff at Georgia Tech?"

"No, junior college. I want to design computers someday."

"So," I asked, nodding at my open computer, "what are you doing there?"

"I'm adding more memory and a couple of programs I think you'll like. I also got you a scanner and a color printer," he said, pointing to the far corner of my desk.

I almost hugged him. I'd been bugging my dad for a printer for the longest time. I never thought I'd have a color one.

"There," he said, tightening up a screw on the computer's faceplate. "Looks as good as new, and should work a lot better."

"Thanks," I said, wanting to say more but not really knowing what.

"No problem." He stood, towering over me by about a foot. "Oh, and I want to apologize about earlier with you and your friend. Guess I need to take a change of clothes when I go take a shower. I'm used to being in an all-boys dorm."

"Don't mention it," I said, turning red.

He laughed and walked downstairs.

I knelt by my bed. *Lord, what is going on with me? I've never felt this way about a black guy. I have a boyfriend and I'm in love. God, I'm giving all of this to You. Thank You. I love You.*

I then prayed for Robyn and her family, for Brittany and Branson and Meagan, and for each of my brothers. I prayed for Foster, too, even though we were broken up.

Dinner was sort of weird, with seven of us at the table. Derek ate really fast, with his mouth close to the plate. When he noticed me staring at him, he sat up straighter. "Sorry," he said. "I've been eating cafeteria food for the longest time. A home-cooked meal sure tastes good."

All through dinner, Lance kept asking Derek football questions. Derek answered politely, then started talking about a Christian book he was reading. Liam joined in at that point. Luke had watched Derek fix most of the computers in our house, so he started talking about everything he'd learned.

Derek seemed to fit right in with our family. There was something about him that was bringing us all together. Though his skin was dark, his heart seemed white as the purest snow.

And God answered my prayer. I wasn't looking at Derek as an object anymore. I could see his soul, which was far more appealing than his flesh could ever be.

I was glad Derek had come, and I knew everyone else in my family felt the same way. At that moment we were totally welcoming a stranger.

seeing
another side

brittany stopped me in the hallway between classes. "So, you think I could get some of your time today?" she asked in her usual bossy way.

I loved my friend dearly, but she always acted like her problems were the only ones that existed. I was still feeling dejected about not being able to compete in gymnastics. But she didn't ask me anything about that. Then again, I had sort of abandoned her by hanging out with Robyn. I hadn't even called her all weekend because there'd been so much going on.

"When do you want to talk?" I asked.

"Can you walk me to my next class?"

"Britt, mine is on the other side of the building. I'll be late."

"So blame it on your ankle. Your teacher will give you sympathy. I really, really, really, really need to talk to you."

Against my better judgment, I let her twist my arm.

"My dad's dating again," she said as we headed toward her class. "And I really don't like the lady he's seeing."

I felt like saying, *"You wouldn't like anybody your dad dates."* But she'd probably get mad at me, and I remembered the Bible says we should be slow to speak and quick to listen.

"She's one of his patients. I haven't met her yet, but—"

"Wait a minute." I grabbed her arm and she stopped. "If you haven't even met her, your dad must not be really serious about her. Why are you getting so stressed out?"

"Because I don't want it to get serious." She rolled her eyes at me like I was stupid.

"Why not?" I asked, exasperated.

Brittany hesitated. I sighed, wishing I'd gone ahead to my own class.

"The lady's black, OK?"

I stared at her, trying to picture the situation. "Your father doesn't seem like he's prejudiced. Then again, I do have a hard time imagining him with an African American lady. I mean, it doesn't gross me out or anything, it just seems . . . weird."

"I know!"

We didn't get to finish our conversation, because we got to her class just as the bell rang. I hobbled to my science class. Brittany was right, the teacher didn't say anything about me being tardy.

During the lab, I could tell something was on Robyn's mind. She was doing the work and all, but she seemed distant. I didn't want to pry, but I wanted her to know that if she needed to talk I wanted to listen.

"Hey," I said, placing my hand over hers. "How's your mom?"

Before she could answer, the teacher, Mr. Ide, came by to give me the instructions on what we were supposed to be doing, which I hadn't heard because I'd been late.

When he left Robyn whispered, "The lump is benign."

"That's great!" I hugged her tightly. But she didn't really

respond. "What's wrong?" I asked, letting go of the embrace. "Did they find another lump?"

"My mom's doctor . . . um . . ."

"Yeah?"

"Well, he gave her the good news on Friday, and then he . . . he invited her out to dinner to celebrate. Can you believe that?"

"That's nice. Isn't it?"

"They went out again the next night, and they spent all day Sunday together. Laurel, my mom hasn't dated anybody since my father died. That was ten years ago. So I'm thinking, OK, this is a good thing. Then she asked me how I would feel about her dating a white man. I told her I thought it was sickening. She said she wasn't sure if the relationship would go anywhere, but in case it did, she wanted my approval. I told her no way. Then she said I'd better get my attitude in check. Can you believe that?"

It didn't take a rocket scientist to figure out what was going on. Brittany's dad was a doctor, and he specialized in treating cancer patients.

Brittany's mom and Robyn's dad. It seemed kind of strange at first, but I wasn't opposed to the idea. Mrs. Williams was a tremendous lady. She'd been raising two daughters on her own, just from the royalties on her teen novels and her freelance editing business. And Dr. Cox had taken care of Brittany and her brother after their mom ran off when Brittany was in the eighth grade. The problem was going to be convincing their daughters that this match was possibly made in heaven.

I tried to say some positive things to Robyn, but she threw back negative responses to everything, so I decided to give it a rest.

Later that day, when I was doing homework in my room, my mom walked in. I told her all about Robyn's mom and Brittany's dad. "What am I supposed to do? Shouldn't I try to convince those two that it's OK for their parents to see each other?"

"You're definitely in a unique position. Now, are you absolutely certain they were talking about each other's parents?"

"Robyn's mom is dating a white doctor who works with cancer patients. Brittany's dad is dating a black lady who writes novels." I raised my eyebrows and smirked. "You know anybody else in this town who fits that description?"

"Good point." She sighed. "Well, in the Old Testament God did warn his people not to intermarry with foreigners. But that's because those countries practiced other religions, usually ones that involved abominable practices like ritual prostitution and child sacrifice. The warning had nothing to do with different races, but with conflicting faiths."

"Does the Bible say anything about interracial marriage?" I asked.

"Oh, there are several examples, especially in the Old Testament. In cases where a believer was united with an unbeliever, there was always trouble. But Ruth was a black girl from Moab, and she married Boaz. And Moses married a black woman, Zipporah, who was a Cushite. God even chastised Moses' relatives, Aaron and Miriam, for opposing their union."

That made me feel better. "So I should chastise Brittany and Robyn for opposing their parents' union, right?"

Mom smiled. "Maybe you just need to pray for God to soften their hearts."

I knew she was right. There wasn't anything I could do to change their minds, but God could. This problem wasn't mine to solve.

As soon as my mom left, I prayed for Brittany and Robyn. I prayed they would have God's perspective, not the world's. If they did, I knew their harsh thoughts toward their parents would go away.

The following Friday after school, I came home to an empty house. My brothers were helping my parents set up for Teen Friday, our church's Memorial Day weekend dance. I had decided to go, even though my ankle was still a little sore. I'd invited Brittany, Meagan, and Robyn to come too; they all said they'd try to make it.

I checked the mail carefully, hoping to find an acceptance letter from UGA. I felt confident that if they accepted me, God would find some way to cover the finances. But waiting for the acceptance letter was driving me crazy.

When I walked into the living room, I saw a shirtless Derek doing push-ups on the floor. He must have done fifty of them in about thirty seconds. I was blown away.

All of a sudden he collapsed and grabbed his left shoulder, his face contorted in pain. He crawled over to a little glass jar on a side table. He poured out some oil and rubbed it into his shoulder. Then he knelt to pray.

When he stood up, he saw me and jumped back. "How long have you been there?"

He reached for his white T-shirt and pulled it on over his muscular torso, sweat immediately soaking through the thin cotton.

"I'm sorry. I should have said something, but you were working out and praying and all."

"No problem," he said, wiping his damp forehead.

"Hey, can I ask you something?"

"Sure."

I picked up the jar of oil. "I saw you put this on your shoulder. Did the doctor give it to you?"

"No, it's . . ." He took the bottle from me. "It's oil that's been anointed. My mom fasted and prayed over it, then had the pastor at church and some of my aunts pray over it too. I believe God wants me well, and this is a symbol to remind me that God's in control."

"Do you have an injury?" I asked, sitting on the couch.

"Yes," he said, joining me. "Last season, I tore my

ligament sacking a quarterback. I've got to be able to block one-on-one, and my opponent can't know that I have a weakness. Right now everybody thinks I'm going to be less than my best next year. I feel my shoulder getting stronger every now and then. But I know I'm not a hundred percent. What you just saw me do was my way of taking the healing out of my hands and giving it back to God."

"What if He doesn't heal you?" I asked.

"Then He'll heal my desire to be healed."

That was deep thinking, but I understood it. I longed to go to the Olympics, but thanks to my ankle injuries, my chances were next to nothing. Still, I hoped that God would work out a way. If He didn't, I felt confident He had something better in mind for me.

"Do you think I could try it?" I asked. The concept really appealed to me. I'd still do the exercises my doctor recommended to heal my ankle, but anointing it, praying over it, and giving it to God sounded like a comforting thought.

Derek unwrapped my Ace bandage, put three drops of oil on my swollen ankle, and rubbed it in. As he rubbed he sang an old hymn. He couldn't really carry a tune or stay on key, but there was something about the way he sang that was filled with passion.

"Guide my feet, Lord, while I run this race. Guide my feet, Lord, while I run this race. Guide my feet, Lord, while I run this race. 'Cause I don't want to run in vain."

Then he started praying. When he finished, my ankle really did feel better. I couldn't explain why, but it did.

As he began to massage my ankle again, the front door opened and I heard Branson's voice. "What's going on here? Who's this guy rubbing your leg?"

Derek and I turned around and saw Branson with Lance.

"Hey, man, he's cool," my brother told my boyfriend. "That's Derek Maddox. He's staying with us for the summer."

"Derek Maddox?" Branson said, his eyes wide. "Starting linebacker for Georgia Tech?"

Derek stood and shook Branson's hand. "Yeah, that's me."

"Wow, I really respect your moves," Branson said. "But, hey, you can't be moving in on my girl."

"He was just showing me how to make my leg better," I said, rewrapping the bandage.

"I didn't know you had a boyfriend, Laurel," Derek said. "Seems like he cares about you a lot."

"Yeah," I said. I hopped over to Branson and pulled him outside. "What is wrong with you?" I asked after the door closed.

"How was I supposed to know who the guy was? I come into your house and I see some black dude rubbing your leg, and you're all relaxed like you're enjoying it."

"We were praying."

"Oh. Well, I'm sure he's cool but . . . come on, it caught me off guard."

I kissed him on the cheek. "You were jealous."

He laughed and put his arms around my waist. "Are we going out tonight?"

"I've got to go to that dance at church. I already invited Brittany and Meagan and Robyn."

"Then I'll go too."

"Well, it *is* your church, so you should. But I need to get there early to set up, and I'll probably have to stay late to help clean."

Branson played with my waist. "I'll just meet you there then. But save me a dance, all right?"

"Of course."

"And don't go flirting with that Georgia Tech boy."

"Don't worry." I kissed his cheek again and he kissed me on the lips. The moment sucked me in and I didn't want to be rescued.

After a few minutes he whispered, "I'll see you tonight." I watched him get in the car and peel out. Part of my heart went with him. I was sure crazy about that guy.

"I didn't mean to get you in trouble with your boyfriend," Derek said as I came back into the house. He sat alone on the couch with his Bible on the table beside him.

"Oh, no, things are fine."

"Yeah, I could see that. You two were pretty intense."

"Were you watching me?" I asked.

He shrugged. "Kinda. Like when you were watching me work out." He seemed a little irritated.

"And was there something wrong with what you saw?"

"I don't know. For a relationship to work, people have to be on the same page. It seemed to me you were sending him a message that—"

"I don't know what you're getting at, but our relationship is—" I felt heat rise to my cheeks. "You know what? I don't have to talk to you about my love life. It's none of your business. I don't even know you."

"Look, I'm just making an observation, as a brother in Christ." He stood. "A relationship can get a little crazy when people think they're supposed to take it to the next level. I just think you ought to watch yourself, that's all. You can take my advice or not, whatever you want." He started to leave the room.

"Now, you hold on a minute," I said. "I have something to say to you."

He stopped and turned.

"You're staying at my house because my dad invited you. But that doesn't mean you can get all in my life and everything."

"Laurel, I don't know why I'm here. The opportunity came up, and nothing else was working out for me, so it seemed like this was where God wanted me. I asked Him why He wanted me to go live with a white family. But now that I'm here, I'm starting to see why. I'm not perfect or anything, but I need to tell you guys about some things. You call yourselves a Christian family, but some of the things you're all doing aren't right. If you're trying to live God's way, there are certain things you shouldn't do."

I felt intensely frustrated and I didn't know why. Part of me knew he was right but I didn't want to hear it. I hurried out of the room. Halfway up the stairs I landed on my left foot too hard and squealed.

"You need help?" he asked, standing at the foot of the stairs.

"No, I'm fine." Frustrated even more, I grabbed the rail and hopped up to my room. The minute I got there I heard my family come home.

"Come on, Laurel," Dad called. "We've got to eat quickly so you can get to the dance."

When we were all sitting at the dinner table, everyone started talking to Derek. But that Goody Two-shoes guy had bothered me so much I ate my baked chicken and mashed potatoes in complete silence.

At the dance, Branson and I had a great time, but I couldn't stop thinking about what Derek had said. Branson kept grabbing my waist, even when we weren't dancing, and nuzzling my neck.

Robyn didn't show up, and neither did Brittany, but Meagan came. The minute I saw her, I asked Branson to get us some refreshments so I could talk to her privately.

"Laurel," she moaned the minute we were alone, "I don't know what to do."

"What do you mean?"

"I still like both of your brothers." She looked across the room at my oldest brother. "Liam is so creative and talented and . . . good." She turned her gaze to a different corner. "But Lance is athletic and attractive and . . . well, a bad boy. And I kinda like that." She groaned. "Do you hate me?"

"No," I said. "I understand. Really."

I looked at Branson, goofing around with some guys at the refreshment table. Then I gazed at Foster, who was dancing with Shaney, the sophomore gymnastics chick. But I didn't see any trace of passion there. They seemed to be enjoying each other, but five people could have fit between the two of them.

Branson came up and handed me a glass of punch. Then he wrapped his arm around my waist and kissed my ear. It felt so good I let myself get lost in it for a second. Then I jerked away. "Branson, stop."

"Oh, you're right," he said. "We're in church." He laughed.

The rest of the night he behaved like a perfect gentleman, but I could tell he wanted more from me. And a part of me wanted to give him more.

Lord, I prayed, *these thoughts aren't Your thoughts. Help me.*

After the dance ended, Branson helped clean up the place. He asked to take me home, but my dad said since it was late I should go home with the family. I felt kinda relieved because I knew if I were alone with Branson I couldn't trust myself to stay pure. It really made me sick to realize that Derek was right.

"So, how come Brittany gets to spend the night at your house and I can't?" Meagan wailed at me over the phone the next day.

I was really mad that Brittany had opened her big mouth and told Meagan I'd invited her over.

"You don't love me anymore," she accused. "Just because I'm torn between your brothers, you're going to hold that against me."

"Meg, that's not it at all."

"Then why does she get invited and I don't?"

I heard Brittany's voice as she snatched the phone away from Meagan. "I told her not to call you. If you wanted her to come, you would have told her. First rule of etiquette, never beg to be invited to something. But she wouldn't listen to me."

"Thanks for telling her, Brittany," I said sarcastically.

"I didn't know you just wanted to hang out with me."

"I wouldn't say that."

"Laurel, you don't have to explain. She'll be OK. I'll take her to get her nails done. Now, what time do you want me over?"

"Around five?"

"Works for me."

"Can I speak to Meagan again?"

Brittany didn't answer, but Meagan came back on. "Yes?" she said in a pouty voice.

"I just wanted to say I'm sorry. I don't want you to think that I didn't want you over at my house or anything."

"Well, what else am I supposed to think?" Her whining turned to anger.

I couldn't tell her my plans for Brittany that evening. She might misunderstand, or worse, tip Brittany off and have her decide not to show up. Even though the issue between my brothers wasn't the main reason I didn't want Meagan to come, I said, "It's gonna take some time to work out all this stuff between Lance and Liam."

"Yeah, I understand. You and Britt have fun. I'll be fine. Don't worry about me. But you hurt my feelings and that's not fair."

I heard a click and a dial tone. I felt bad, but I had to put my plan into action. I'd make it up to Meagan later. I hung up and called Robyn.

"Hey, girl," she said. "Sorry I couldn't make it to your church thing last night. My mom had a date and she made me watch my little sister. Then Jackson came over and I had to read him all up and down. That boy tried to play me, still claiming that you wanted him. I read his tracks myself, figured him all out, so he spilled it and said you had too much to drink."

"What?" I shrieked. "Robyn, you know that's a lie, right?"

"Yeah, I know. Jackson is such a loser. I'm getting tired of him. He could sense he wasn't all that with me anymore, and Laurel, you would have thought he'd never had any of this, that's how sweet he was acting. You know what I'm talking about?"

"I think so. But can we talk about it more later? You're still going to spend the night over here, right?"

"Oh, I'll be there. You can count on it," she said, as if I'd just offered her a prime rib dinner.

"Why'd you say it like that?"

"Because of that fine houseguest you have over there, girl. What I saw in that towel last week could make me totally forget about Jackson."

I didn't have the courage to tell her that Derek wasn't going to be at our house that night. He had to go bail his druggie mom out of jail . . . again.

After we said good-bye I started straightening my room. Brittany and Robyn had one thing in common: They were both neat freaks. I knew I needed some polishing in that area, and the last thing I wanted them to do was rag on me about my untidiness.

Mom brought in the vacuum cleaner with a sly smile. "So, what's your plan, Little Miss Friend-maker?"

"Friend-maker? What's that?"

"Something like a matchmaker, but with two girl-friends."

"Oh, Mom," I groaned, thinking about the song "Match-maker, Matchmaker" from *Fiddler on the Roof*. Then an idea hit me.

"Hey, that's it! I want to play the *Fiddler on the Roof* video tonight. The couples in that movie got married even though their father didn't want them to, but then he realized that love was the only important thing. Not religions, cultures, income, status, or even race. If God's in the relationship, it can work out. Maybe Robyn and Brittany will get that from the movie."

"Well, I hope you know what you're getting into."

"I do. The only reason I'm doing this is because I care a lot about both of them."

Five o'clock came, and neither of my friends had arrived. I sat in my room, twiddling my thumbs, cleaning things I'd already cleaned, and telling myself they weren't going to show. At five forty-six the doorbell rang. When I opened it, they were both standing there, overnight bags in hand. I could tell they were extremely surprised to see each other there.

"Come in, guys. Let's go up to my room."

"I need to go to the bathroom," Robyn said with a slight wink. She scurried down the hall. Brittany stormed straight upstairs in a huff, without even saying hello. Robyn looked back at me, her eyes asking me to follow her. I joined her in the guest bathroom.

"Brittany obviously wants to talk to you about something. So I'm willing to give you two some time alone. We've got the rest of the night to gab. Meanwhile, I can wait down here and be entertained by your houseguest." She raised her eyebrows twice.

Before I could respond I heard Brittany yelling at the top of her lungs. "Laurel, come up here!"

"Hold on," I said to Robyn, "I'll be right back."

I ran upstairs. "Please don't yell, Britt. We aren't the only ones here, you know."

"Why is that black girl at your house? That is so rude. I hate when people just drop by unannounced. Tell her I'm spending the night and she needs to go."

This wasn't going to be easy. I dragged Brittany downstairs, where Robyn was sitting on the couch, tapping her toes on the carpet.

"OK, guys," I said, looking at both of my friends. "I'm just going to come out and say this. I invited both of you over here to spend the night tonight."

"What?" they both said at the same time.

"If she's staying, I'm leaving," Brittany said, her arms crossed.

"You don't have to leave," Robyn said with a sneer. "The person I came to visit isn't even here. And I don't have time to be around fake people."

"I think both of you guys are being pretty selfish. Robyn, you're always calling me racist. Brittany, you act like black people are from Mars, and you don't even try to get to know them. But you two have a lot in common. One thing especially, and that's your parents."

They stared at me and then at each other. Gradually I saw them figure out what I was saying.

My mom came in with three glasses of lemonade and a plate of peanut butter cookies. After setting everything on the coffee table, she closed her eyes and folded her hands. "Lord, I pray for this evening and ask that You be here with these girls. Amen."

The mood softened some. After Mom left I asked, "Either of you guys seen *Fiddler on the Roof?*" Neither of them had, so I popped in the video.

After it was over Robyn asked, "Was I supposed to get some kind of message out of that?"

"Well—"

"My mom ain't white," Robyn interrupted, "and she ain't no Jew. That flick ain't about me."

"That flick ain't about me," Brittany mimicked.

Robyn stood, her left hand on her hip. "What you trying to say?" she said, wagging a finger at Brittany. "That I don't know how to talk proper English? Please! You think you know everything about black people but you don't know nothing, you prejudiced cracker."

Brittany stood almost nose-to-nose with Robyn. "Don't make me use the one word that I know will bring you over the edge," she threatened.

I stepped between them. "Guys," I begged, "can't you just get over your personal feelings and start seeing another side?"

s e v e n

receiving
top praise

you better get your little white finger out of my face," Robyn warned.

"Ooh, I'm shaking," Brittany responded.

"Stop it," I screamed. "I didn't invite you guys over for you to attack each other. Robyn, you're acting like a drama queen, and Brittany, you're behaving like a spoiled brat. Can you both just lose the attitude and try to get along?"

"I know she doesn't like me," Brittany said, snarling at Robyn. "I see the way she looks at me."

"You think everybody's beneath you," Robyn said. "I don't like you, and you'd best believe I don't want my mom dating your dad."

"Ditto that!" Brittany stormed to the other side of the room with her hands folded in her arms.

"Guys, you may not agree on some stuff, but that doesn't mean you can't be friends. At least your parents are dating good people."

Robyn glared at Brittany's back for a long moment, then she turned to me and asked, "So, where's Derek?"

Brittany whirled around. "Who's Derek?"

"He went home for the weekend," I told Robyn.

"And you knew this when?"

"I'm sorry," I said.

"I'm out of here." She started to leave the room.

"Good," Brittany said. "After you leave, Laurel and I can have some fun."

Robyn stopped in her tracks. "Oh, you want me to leave? Then I'm not going anywhere."

"Fine," Brittany said. "You stay here in the living room, and Laurel and I will go upstairs."

I had no clue how to get through to the two of them. So I closed my eyes and started to pray aloud. "Father in heaven," I said, "right now there's a wall between these two people that I can't battle, but I know You can bring it down. I'm sure these girls could get along if all the baggage was out of the way. So I'm asking You right now, Lord, to step in and work all this out. I've run out of ideas to try to make them friends, but I know You can do something special here."

When I opened my eyes and said amen, the two of them echoed the word reverently.

My mom called from the kitchen. "Homemade pizza, anybody?"

Robyn and Brittany glanced at each other, then dashed out of the room. I limped along behind them. "Don't wait for me or anything," I chided them with a grin.

As we ate pizza together, I filled Brittany in on Derek, which got us talking about boys and sports and college. Robyn told Brittany that she had cheered at her old school, Southwest DeKalb High. Brittany admitted that she loved some of their moves, so Robyn showed her a few cheers.

When we moved things up to my room, I asked, "What's really the problem with your parents dating?" Neither of

72

them spoke. "Is the fact that they're not the same color that big a deal?"

"Look, Brittany's dad is an amazing doctor," Robyn said. "I'm really grateful to him for my mom's good news about her cancer. But it's hard being a black woman. Everywhere you go you're either judged or overlooked by white people. I'm all for my mom falling in love again, but she needs somebody who will complement her, and I just don't think Brittany's dad can do that."

I looked at Brittany, who was sitting on my bed. After a moment, she looked at Robyn. "I'm glad my dad was able to help your mom. He's a good doctor. He's a good man, too, and he's been talking about your mom like she's the best thing since his medical degree." She turned to me. "To answer your question, yeah, the race thing is a big issue. My dad goes to the country club and a lot of other places where everybody's white. So if he's going to remarry, it needs to be to someone who can be accepted in his world. Besides, I'd like to have a stepmother who understands me."

"Come on, guys," I pleaded. "I'm sure you and your parents could overcome a few cultural differences."

"You don't understand," Brittany said. "Your mom and dad are together. They're happy. You can't honestly know what it's like when your parents get divorced."

"Or one of them dies," Robyn added.

"And then . . ."

"They marry somebody black," Robyn finished Brittany's sentence. "Or Chinese or Korean or anything other than you are. It's a lot to handle, trust us. We're just normal teenagers, wanting a perfect family. And the way our parents are heading right now is anything but perfect."

"That's right." Brittany looked at Robyn and they both sighed.

In a way my friends were forming a bond, but they were still not in agreement about their parents.

"I'm gonna go take my shower," I said, hoping they'd

take the next step while I was gone. But when I returned, they were actually conspiring to find a way to break their parents up.

"I can't believe you two," I said, sounding like Miss Goody Two-shoes. "You know, nowhere in the Bible does it say that someone can't get married to a person of another race. God can work this out. Give it to Him and let Him sort it out."

Brittany shook her head. "Laurel, my relationship with God is kinda rocky right now. He's in my life, but I'm not ready to do everything His way just yet."

"Tell me about it, girl," Robyn said, emphasizing her comment with dramatic hand gestures. "Even after my dad died, my mom kept writing Christian books like God was still there. You really think God's gonna work out my dad's death to my advantage? That's just sick."

I fell onto the bed. "What have I done?" I groaned.

Brittany looked at me with compassion. "Don't be mad. We're glad you got us together. Now we can plan a good strategy to break our parents up."

"Without either of them getting hurt," Robyn added.

Brittany grinned at her. "Right!"

Robyn wagged her finger at me and smiled. "You know, you might just get a new outfit out of this one."

I put my hands over my face and shook my head. I didn't want to be thanked for creating this mess.

"Dang, you kiss good," Branson said to me under the steps at school a couple of weeks later. I didn't want to pull my lips away. I could have held him close to me forever, but then the bell rang.

He jogged away, apparently not caring if I made it to my class on time. "I've got a test today," he yelled over his shoulder.

I could have punched him in the stomach.

As I turned to go to class, I ran smack into Foster Mc-Dowell. He looked at me like I'd done something terribly wrong. I could tell he'd seen me kissing Branson.

"What?" I asked.

"Nothing."

"You got something you want to say?"

"Hey, it's your life, so do whatever you want."

He started walking away, but I pulled him back. "Obviously, you want to say something to me. So talk."

He shook his head. "You're in the same place doing the same thing that you broke up with that guy for before. His hands were all over you."

"You don't have to be jealous, Foster. You and I aren't together anymore. So move on. You flaunt your girlfriend in my face enough."

"Laurel, it's not jealousy. When you were my girlfriend, I respected you a lot more than that. Sex wasn't the only thing on my mind. I wanted to be with you, and be there for you. Seems to me Branson only wants to be with you for one reason, and from what I can see, you're on the same track."

Part of me wanted to lash out at Foster and tell him my life was none of his business. But then I realized he cared for me. He cared enough to put up with me ridiculing him and telling him to butt out. Our relationship, though short, had been deep because it was built on Christian principles, and though we weren't dating anymore, our core beliefs were the same. I guess he felt it was his duty to let me know that I was going astray.

I nibbled at the inside of my lip, swallowed my pride, and said, "Thanks. I appreciate your concern for me. It's just that I really like the feelings that soar through my body when Branson touches my face or holds my hand or touches my back or—"

"Let's just say, gets physical."

I blushed suddenly. "I can't believe I'm talking to you about this."

"I don't want you to do something you'll regret." Foster started telling me about the qualities he adored in me. None of them had anything to do with my body or sexual desires.

"Your compliments are too much," I told him.

"It's just the truth."

I hadn't thought it was possible that the two of us could be friends. But Foster asked if I wanted to sit somewhere and talk. My ankle was throbbing, so I suggested we go to the outdoor lunch area.

"Hey, I heard about you not being able to go to Georgia because of your ankle," Foster said.

"Actually, I'm still hoping I'll be able to," I said, although I hadn't received my official letter of acceptance. I knew I wanted to go to Georgia, even if I had to get a school loan or something. The question was, did Georgia want me?

"That's great," Foster said. "I hope you get to go."

"What about you? Have you decided on any place?"

"Yeah, I'm going to USC."

My heart stopped for a second. "In California?"

"I lived there my whole life, until I moved here last year, so I applied for a scholarship and got one. I've still got lots of friends back there."

"When are you leaving?"

"Pretty soon after graduation." Foster looked into my eyes. "Laurel, I don't want to leave without us being friends."

"I'd like that," I said.

"If Branson really cares about you, he won't push you into something you don't want to do. I'm just not sure how long Branson's going to wait. He's the type of guy who expects certain things in a relationship. I hear him bragging in the locker room all the time. When you return his advances, you make him think that's what you want."

"But what I'm displaying to Branson is kind of what I feel. I think that's why you and I didn't make it. I felt a little neglected when you didn't want to kiss me or hold my hand. When I did something that made you go against your morals, I felt bad. But the truth is, I'm not as perfect as I want to be. I mean, I don't want to have sex, but I do kinda want to. I'm scared to death of doing it, and I know the Lord doesn't want me to. But I love the guy, and I love the way he makes me feel."

Foster touched my shoulder. "I'll be praying for you, Laurel. The answer you need is in Jesus Christ. You've got to run away from temptation, not toward it."

I gave him the biggest friendship hug I could. "Thanks for caring enough to tell me the tough stuff."

The next day at the last student assembly of the year, the principal recognized all the seniors' achievements. I got an award for A/B honor roll and another one for being the MVP of our gymnastics team. Then Foster and I each received a medal of honor for our bravery during the shooting last fall. I didn't feel particularly heroic about that day. I had frozen in the hallway and just watched.

The principal handed the microphone to Foster.

"I told you guys how I felt right after the incident," he said, "so I'm going to let Laurel speak this time."

Being put on the spot made me nervous, but I knew the Lord wanted me to convey something to my classmates. I didn't know what it was when I took the microphone, but as I listened to the Holy Spirit, words flowed out.

"That day in the hallway I didn't move because I was afraid I'd get shot. At first, I had the coldest heart I ever thought I could have. I was mad at the administration for not having enough security, I was mad at the gunman for doing this to our school. I was even mad at myself because in that moment, when I could have taken my last breath, I realized there was so much in life that I wished I had done. But if that was going to be my final moment, I had no chance to go back and do it all over again. I couldn't blame anybody for that but me. I had a good friend who was going through some crazy stuff then, and I wasn't there for her like I wanted to be. I knew I needed to quote Scriptures to get her through that whole thing because she was so scared, but I couldn't remember any. I hadn't really been studying God's Word."

I looked at Brittany and saw tears in her eyes.

"I thought about my parents that day too," I continued. "I'd been growing further away from them instead of soaking up the knowledge they had for my life. If I'd been shot that day, I wouldn't have had the chance to let them know how much I loved them."

I noticed Robyn staring up at me. I knew she was thinking about her father, wishing she'd had more years with him.

"Being honored here today for my courage during that moment is really hard to accept. But if I can say anything to you guys, it would be to live every day to the fullest, and live it for the Lord. Next year, I'll be on my own. But it's sure been nice having parents and the high school administration to lean on."

I locked eyes with Dr. Wood for a moment. She was smiling at me.

"Pray all the time and work really hard. If you have a heart for God, everything else will fall in place. Maybe not the way you want it to, but in whatever way God knows is best."

"I can't believe it's your graduation day," Mom said as she stared at me in the mirror in my room. "I still remember the morning I sent you off to kindergarten."

Mom picked up the brush from the counter and started brushing my long hair. I watched a tear fall down her cheek. Though I didn't say so very often, I thought my mom was beautiful. I'd always hated that I didn't have her blond hair and blue eyes, like Lance did. Brittany looked more like my mother than I did. I took after Dad, and so did my other brothers.

"Mom, don't cry. You're too pretty to be sad."

"You're the one with the gorgeous light brown hair like your dad's sister."

"I wish I could have known her," I said. My Aunt Charlie had died in college from a drug overdose. My parents always told me she was smart and a good person. She just got mixed up with the wrong people.

"Your dad's been thinking about Charlie a lot lately, now that you're about to go off to college."

"Does that scare him?"

"I think it makes him a little nervous."

"Mom, I'm going to be fine," I said.

"I know."

"I promise, the only people I'll hang out with are those who know the Lord."

Mom put the brush down, her eyes watery. I held her hand, then threw my arms around her and hugged her as if I would never see her again. She hugged back even tighter. "I'm going to miss you more than you will ever know."

While we were still hugging, someone banged on the door.

"Hon," my father's voice said, "could you let me in? I've got something for Laurel."

When Mom opened the door, I saw my dad holding an envelope with the University of Georgia emblem on the upper left-hand corner. A big smile was plastered across his face. My grandparents, who had flown in for my graduation ceremony, were all gathered behind him, smiling equally as big.

My dad waved the already opened envelope in the air. "You're in, my girl."

My heart skipped a beat. "They accepted me?"

"Of course they did," he said, handing me the proof.

I grabbed the envelope and held it close to my chest. Then reality struck and I flopped onto the bed. "What about the money?" I asked.

Dad glanced at Mom, then looked at the floor, his shoulders slumped. "Your mother and I talked about it a lot, honey, and we just don't see how we can afford—"

"But we can," my Grandma Ma butted in.

"Your grandma and I have decided to cover your first year's tuition," my mom's father said, beaming.

"And we're going to pay for all your books," my other grandmother said.

"Really?" I said, barely breathing.

"That's right, honey," my other grandpa confirmed.

Dad looked up from the floor with a mischievous grin.

"There's a packet of information in the living room from UGA about classes, scheduling, orientation, sororities, and all that," Mom told me, sounding almost as excited as I felt.

I looked around at all these wonderful people who loved me, amazed at how much God had blessed me.

"But . . . why didn't you tell me before?" I asked.

"We wanted to wait for the acceptance letter," Dad said. "Just in case . . ."

I jumped up and gave my dad a big wet kiss on his forehead. My pink lipstick smeared off on his face. He looked in the mirror at the imprint as if it were the best thing that had happened to him in a long while. I handed him a tissue because I didn't want him going to my graduation with a big lipstick stain on his forehead.

Then I went around and gave great big hugs to Mom and all of my grandparents.

"It feels like I'm losing my baby girl," Dad said.

My mom stopped even trying to hold back her tears.

When everyone left to let me finish getting ready for graduation, I got down on my knees and thanked the Lord for working things out for me. "God, I am so humbled right now. And so thankful. Help me not to be as stubborn and stupid as I was as a high schooler. Help me figure out Your plan for my life. I never want to let You down. Amen."

When I walked across the stage that afternoon, I felt like I was really worth something.

After the ceremony I found Kirsten and gave her a big hug. "I can't believe this might be the last time I'll see you," I said.

"Promise you'll write to me," she said, tears in her eyes.

"I will," I said, not wanting to let go of her. "And promise me you'll find a gym up there in New York so you can keep up with your gymnastics. You've got too much talent to let it go to waste."

"I hope I find a friend like you in New York," she said.

"You might be out of luck there," I said, trying to relieve the somber mood before we both fell apart. "I'm one of a kind, you know."

"You sure are," she said, chuckling a little in spite of her tears. She released me and wiped her wet cheeks. "Look, I've got to say good-bye to a lot of people today. I'll call you as soon as I get to New York."

"You'd better," I said with a grin.

As she took off to go cry with some other friends, I saw Brittany and Robyn walking hand in hand, laughing and giggling. "You guys are acting like sisters," I said. "What am I missing?"

"We're acting," Brittany said. "For our parents. As soon as we all get to dinner tonight, we're going to start messing up their relationship."

"How do you plan to do that?"

"We can't tell you right now," Robyn said. "You'll hear all about it later."

As I watched them walk off arm in arm, Branson came up to me. He looked so handsome in his maroon graduation gown with the gold sash. "We're free," he said, swinging me around. "We're adults now."

"I got my acceptance letter to Georgia," I squealed.

"I got mine yesterday."

"Isn't it great?"

"Laurel, this is our night, and I want to make it really special. I'm going to let you know exactly how much I love you." Branson kissed my ear. "Tonight you will experience real love, and you're going to know how it feels receiving top praise."

eɪ ɢ ʜ t

honoring
my father

i don't know if I can go with you tonight," I told Branson. "My dad has a big graduation dinner planned."

"OK," he said. "So you have your family dinner, and later I'll come by the restaurant to pick you up. Then the magic can begin." He ran his fingers through my hair and whispered, "You're gonna love making love to me."

Before I could say anything, Derek showed up. "What's going on here? Excuse me. Distance. Distance." He cut between Branson and me. I was relieved that I didn't have to respond to the comment that sent chills up my spine.

"What are you doing?" Branson complained.

Derek looked me in the eye and whispered, "Your family's coming."

Branson whirled around. "Oh, Reverend Shadrach, hello, sir."

"Congratulations, son," my father said. "I assume you two were talking about plans for this evening."

Inside I screamed, *Please say no, Dad. Say we can't go out tonight!*

"We've got a nice dinner planned, but I don't want you to think I'm an old fuddy-duddy. You guys can go out after dinner."

Branson grinned from ear to ear and pumped my dad's hand. "Thank you, sir." Then he kissed me on the cheek. "Looks like it's gonna be our night after all," he whispered. "Should I pick her up at the house, sir?"

"That would be fine. We should be home around seven."

At dinner my grandmothers hugged me really tightly, and my granddads gave a few words of encouragement.

My brothers handed me an envelope with three hundred dollars in it, one hundred from each of them. "This is for you," Liam said, "to buy whatever you want for college. We know we give you a hard time but we're really going to miss you."

"Thanks for being such great brothers," I said, hugging each of them.

After the waiter took our orders, everyone became engulfed in various conversations. Derek, who was sitting beside me, said, "Your boyfriend is really putting some pressure on you, isn't he? He wants to take things all the way."

"Did you overhear us?" I hissed.

"Oh, I didn't have to hear a word."

"What did you do, read his lips?"

"No. It was his body language, his attitude. The way he looked at you like you were already his. It's trouble, Laurel. Personally I don't think you should go out with him tonight."

"He's my boyfriend, Derek. Eventually we're going to have to deal with that. But we're nowhere near that point yet. Thanks for your advice, but I'll be OK."

When we returned to the house, Branson was sitting in his blue Camaro, waiting at the curb. He was wearing a black tank top, and the muscles on his arms made me more excited than I'd ever been with him. I zipped into the house and changed into a short black skirt and a sparkly pink blouse with spaghetti straps, freshened my makeup, and brushed my hair. Deciding to leave my crutches at home, I limped back out to Branson's car, where my dad was chatting with my boyfriend.

"Have her home by midnight," Dad told Branson. "We're going to a late show at the movies, and that's about when we'll be back."

"Yes, sir," Branson said with a huge smile.

A half-hour later, when he pulled up to the Ritz Carlton and stepped out of the car for valet parking, I realized that Derek had been right. I was crazy to let myself get into this situation. But now that I was in it, I didn't know how to graciously get out of it.

When we got up to the room Branson had rented for the night, he touched my hair, kissed me on the shoulder, and slid my blouse strap down. Before I knew it I was standing in front of him wearing just my bra and skirt. At that moment pleasing God didn't seem as important as pleasing Branson. When his lips touched my neck, desire consumed me.

"I love you," I murmured.

"I love you," he replied. "I'm sorry for all that stuff I put you through. When you weren't in my life, I realized the mistakes I made. Now that I have another chance, I want to show you how much I care. We're adults now. We don't have to play with this love thing. We can really let it all out."

As he slid his hands over my skin, my heart started pounding. He kissed me and led me to the king-sized bed. When my head hit the pillow, I started kissing him back.

He was gorgeous and he loved me. I wanted him to know that he really mattered to me, that he didn't need anyone else to satisfy him. As he unbuttoned my skirt I said, "What about—"

He covered my lips with his finger. "I've got protection. Hold on."

He stood up and dug into his jeans pocket. When he

pulled out a foil-wrapped condom, the enjoyment started turning to nervousness. I thought I'd wanted to go all the way, but suddenly a tear started forming in my eye.

"Laurel, what's wrong?" Branson asked as he joined me again on the bed. "Why are you crying?"

I started shaking all over and I turned away from him.

"I thought you wanted to be with me," he said. He didn't sound angry, just extremely disappointed.

I didn't know what I was feeling. But I could imagine God looking at what I was doing and not being happy with what He saw. What Branson thought mattered to me, but not as much as pleasing the Lord. I had disappointed Him. Even though the act hadn't been committed, I had gone way too far with Branson.

"I'm sorry," I groaned through my tears. "I'm so sorry."

Branson held me in a tender embrace. "It's OK," he said as he gently kissed my forehead. He stroked my hair, calming me down. It felt so good, I ended up drifting off to sleep. When I woke up, Branson was still holding me.

"I'm sorry," I said again, getting up and putting my blouse back on. "I guess I'm just not ready."

"I'm sorry; I thought you were," he replied.

"I do love you. And I really want you. But I want to honor the Lord."

"Do you think it makes God angry when two adults show their love to each other?"

"I don't think it pleases Him when two people who aren't married take things too far. I love you a lot. But I can't give you what you want. If you want to break up with me, I'll understand."

I half expected him to get up and walk out the door, but he didn't. He just kept holding me. When the clock said eleven, Branson drove me home. The ride was extremely awkward. Neither of us said a word.

When we pulled onto my street, I saw Lance standing on our front lawn with two big black men. The taller one was holding a baseball bat, and the shorter one was holding my brother.

"Oh, my gosh," I cried. "What's happening?"

Branson drove faster and almost ran into the one with the bat. The guy turned and glared at Branson, then smashed his hood with the bat.

I jumped out and made a dash for the front door, but as I reached the first porch step, someone grabbed me from behind. I slipped on the stair, my ankle twisting. "Help!" I screamed. Then I remembered. My family had gone to a late-night movie. They wouldn't be back until around midnight.

"Leave my sister alone," Lance shouted.

The shorter black guy, who had previously been holding my brother, was now holding me. "Dang, Lance," he purred. "I didn't know yo' sistah was so fine."

"Get your hands off my girlfriend," Branson hollered. I turned and saw the guy with the baseball bat smearing my boyfriend's face up against the dented hood of his car.

"Why are you doing this?" I screamed. "I thought Lance paid you guys."

"Yeah, right." My attacker threw me into Lance's arms. "Yo' dumb brothah been avoidin' our calls. So me and my pal Vincent here decided to pay him a little visit . . . after yo' folks left, o' course."

The front door of my house burst open. Derek stood on the porch, light from the entryway silhouetting his muscular frame.

"What dat guy doin' here, JQ?" the one holding Branson against the car asked. "I thought you said nobody was home."

"Brothah, you better back up." JQ grabbed me by the arm and Lance by the back of the neck.

"Hold on, now," Derek said, walking slowly down the steps. "I'm just coming to talk to you. Don't do anything crazy."

When Derek came near, JQ said, "Hey, man, don't I know you? You look like a pro ball player."

"I'm a student at Georgia Tech."

"Yeah," he said with sudden recognition. "You that Derek Maddox guy. Linebacker, right? You flat-out tight, yo! What you doin' here?"

"I'm staying with these nice people for the summer. Now, what's going on here?"

"This boy ain't been true to his word," JQ grumbled, shoving Lance toward Derek. "He ain't paid what he owes."

"Look," Vincent said, "I like dis li'l white boy an' all. He got heart. We jus' tryin' to get paid up here. He go back on his word, see, so he get hurt. I gotta make a example out o' him, ya know. I gave him thirty days to pay me and I ain't seen jack."

"I'll work something out," Derek said. "You can take my word. We'll come up with a payment plan that'll make everybody happy."

Branson mumbled something as he tried to lift his head up from the car. I didn't hear what it was, but it must have been a smart comment because Vincent punched his face back down on the hood.

"Come on," Derek said. "We don't need all this violence. Now, let me borrow Lance for a minute."

JQ hesitated. "Awright, man," he finally said.

Derek and Lance walked toward the front door, which was still open. JQ leered at me. I stepped back, but he yanked me closer. He smelled of sweat, hair gel, cigarettes, and beer. Not a pleasant combination. I tried to wriggle free of his grasp, but he was too strong for me. His eyes were filled with lust, and he grinned at me with yellow teeth. His alcohol-and-nicotine breath almost made me gag.

"OK," Derek said from the porch. "We've got it worked out. Lance is in the house right now getting my wallet. He's gonna pay you five hundred dollars cash tonight, and two hundred dollars a week until he's free and clear. If he misses a payment, I'll be good for it."

"No way," JQ growled. "That'll take forever. I want four grand now, jus' for havin' to go to the extra trouble to collect."

Lance came out of the house. "You only have four hundred dollars."

"Don't you got some money, punk?" Vincent growled at Branson. He reached into my boyfriend's back pocket and took out his wallet. With one hand, he flipped it open, pulled out the cash, and tossed the wallet into the hedges. "Got 'bout a hundred twenty-five dollars here," he said, thumbing through the bills.

Suddenly remembering the graduation gift my brothers had given me, I said, "I have some money. It's in my purse in the car."

JQ shoved me toward the passenger seat. "Get it," he ordered.

I reached into the car, pulled out my purse, and gave him the envelope that held the three hundred dollars.

"That's about eight hundred now. You might just live after all," JQ said to Lance.

"Come on," my brother pleaded. "Let my family go. I'll pay back the rest of the money you loaned me. I promise."

JQ squinted at Lance. "But how am I gonna get compensated for my extra trip?" He peered at Derek. "Tell ya what. How 'bout we get some tickets to one o' yo' games?"

Derek took in a deep breath. "Man, we don't get many tickets."

JQ grabbed my arm again.

"I might be able to get you into one game," Derek said quickly.

"Oh, it ain't jus' gonna be for me, bro. I wanna come in there with my whole posse. I need eight tickets, dog, in the good section. I wanna be sittin' right by them fancy white alumni, eatin' all dat caviar and stuff."

Derek shook his head. "I'll see what I can do."

"You better, man." Vincent turned to Lance. "And you better pay me da whole six grand. Ya got four days to come up with the first two hundred. If my money ain't on time, this deal is off."

JQ released my arm and nodded at Vincent. "Come on, dog, let's go." As he passed Derek, he pointed his finger in his face. "Don't you go forgettin' my tickets, boy." He hopped into a shiny black SUV parked at the curb.

I dashed into Derek's arms, thanking him over and over. Then I heard a derisive laugh. I turned around and realize that Vincent hadn't released Branson.

"Hey, man, look like dat boy's stealin' yo' girl from you. And he ought to be able to take care o' dat, 'cause yo' punk behind is weak, man." The guy released Branson, but when my boyfriend started to stand up, Vincent popped him in the face with his fist. Branson fell to the ground. I ran over to him as Vincent joined JQ and they sped away.

I tried to help Branson up, but he was so frustrated and embarrassed he pulled away from me. When Derek came over and tried to give him a hand, Branson tackled him. The two of them started wrestling on the ground like children.

"Branson, what's wrong with you?" I asked.

"Hey, if he don't want to get hit again, he better get off of me," Derek warned.

Branson let go of Derek and stood up. "Laurel, do you want to be with this . . . this . . . this black guy?" He said it like he had a problem with Derek that had nothing to do with me.

"Why are you angry at him?" I asked, pointing to Derek, who was getting up off the ground and dusting off his jeans.

"Why are you defending him? You were in his arms a minute ago. I just got my head bashed in by an animal and you ran over to thank him."

"I was just happy that he—that you . . . I was caught up in the moment." I felt so upset I couldn't speak. I just cried.

Derek wandered over to talk to Lance, allowing me and Branson to straighten things out.

"I thought we were trying to work through our issues," Branson said. "You don't want to have sex, and I'm willing to deal with that. I don't want to pressure you. But not supporting me? Making me feel like I'm not able to take care of you? Maybe that Vincent guy was right. Maybe you'll sleep with your houseguest before you sleep with me."

Before I could say anything, he stomped over to Lance. "You'd better settle this debt. We almost got killed tonight because you didn't take care of your business. If you want to be stupid and gamble, use your own money to do it."

Lance glared at him. "You have no right to talk to me like that. You don't know anything about my life."

"I know more than you think." A glimmer of pain shone in Branson's eyes. "I went down that road myself once. I had to get money from my dad to pay off the sharks."

I could tell Lance was surprised, but he still had to act cool. "Yeah, well, my dad doesn't have enough money to just throw it around."

Branson rolled his eyes. "You'd better get a job and quick. Because if I get my butt kicked again for you, if they don't kill you, I might." Branson stormed past me, got in his car, and sped off.

I felt sorry for my boyfriend's bruised ego, but insulting my houseguest, degrading my father, and threatening my brother's life all made me glad I'd said no to him.

When Lance stumbled back into the house, Derek came up to me. "You all right?"

"Yeah. Thanks." I tore my gaze from the direction Branson had gone and looked up at Derek. "If you don't mind my asking, how'd you happen to have four hundred dollars in your wallet?" I knew it was an impolite question, but my curiosity got the better of me.

Derek didn't seem the least bit offended. "I did a computer upgrade this afternoon for my coach. He gave me five hundred dollars for it, but I gave the first hundred to your dad's church." He shrugged. "I'd planned to use the rest to fix up my car, but that can wait."

"You really helped us out today."

"No problem. I'm glad I was here to help." He nodded in the direction Branson had driven off. "Anything else I can do?"

I smiled. "Guess you can't fix everything. I think I just need to be alone for a while."

When he went back inside, I gazed up at the sky. I couldn't say any words, but I knew God was there. Inside I cried, *Lord, please help Branson make it home OK. As angry as I am at him, I do love him. Soften his heart, Lord, and bridge the gap between us. I really want to honor You.*

As two tears fell, a cool summer breeze blew by and dried them. I felt as if God were saying, *"I hear you, Laurel, and I am going to fix this, but I need you to stay on My side."*

Two sets of headlights came up the road—my family coming back home. Dad got out and put his arm around me. "The graduate! How was your evening?"

Confident that my heavenly Father was already solving the problem, I said, "Fine, Dad. Everything was fine." I placed my head on his chest and he walked me inside. It served as a symbol of the Lord saying, *"I've got you snugly in My arms. Rest in Me. Lean on your father and let Me carry your burdens."*

"Thanks, Daddy," I said to my earthy father, talking to my heavenly Father at the same time. "Thank you for being there for me."

Three days later, Lance announced that he'd gotten a job at the Chick-Fil-A in town. Dad was thrilled since the company was run by Christians, and all of Lance's coworkers would be believers. "You'll be equally yoked at work," he observed.

Lance was just glad to have a full-time job for the summer, with a promise to work around his school schedule in the fall.

Realizing how much I needed God's provision, and His perfect timing, I called Mrs. Meaks and told her I wanted to start going to the discipleship group on Thursday nights. She was delighted. I told her I wanted to focus my attention on what was most important in life, which was my relationship with Christ. I figured if I got things in order with the Lord, Branson and UGA and gymnastics would all eventually work out for God's best.

Besides, now that school was over, my schedule was a lot freer. And I couldn't practice gymnastics until my ankle healed. So I had lots of time on my hands, and I didn't want to waste it.

I studied the information booklet from UGA and filled out all the forms. I'd heard mixed opinions about sororities, but Brittany encouraged me to step outside my comfort zone and try new things. I had to admit, the application process seemed grueling. I'd have to arrive on campus a few days early to visit several sororities. After deciding which ones I liked, I had to see if they wanted me. I was concerned about what would happen if I didn't get into the sorority of my choice. But then I figured that even going through it all would be a good experience.

Brittany had decided to go to Florida State because of their cute quarterback, Jett Phillips. Brittany's dad was excited because that was where he went. Somehow she had convinced Meagan to go to Florida with her.

That Thursday I went to the discipleship group. It turned out to be a lot of fun and I really enjoyed myself. But I did notice something that bothered me a little. Everyone in the group was Caucasian. There was not a single person of color in the room.

After everyone else went home, I stuck around to help Mrs. Meaks clean up.

"Laurel, is there something you want to talk about?" she asked.

"Why aren't people really equal?" I blurted out. "When I go to the mall with my girlfriend Brittany, all the store clerks smile at us and we get plenty of assistance. But when I go with my friend Robyn, who's black, sometimes I get looks like, 'Why are you with her?' That just doesn't seem right."

"It's not," she agreed.

"Then a few weeks ago I found out Brittany's dad and Robyn's mom have started seeing each other. Both of my friends think that interracial relationships are hard and their parents shouldn't even try. At first I thought they weren't being fair, that love could conquer all. Both of their parents are saved, and that's what God cares about, not skin color. But the more I think about it, the more I wonder if maybe my friends are right."

"That is a difficult situation."

"Then last week my boyfriend got angry at me because he thought I took a black man's side over his. This guy pretty much saved my life, and he did a really noble thing. I think if he was white, Branson would have been shaking his hand and thanking him for helping me out."

Mrs. Meaks held my hands and started praying. She asked God to give me the wisdom I needed to deal with all these circumstances. When she said "amen," I felt a lot less upset.

The following Sunday, Dad preached a great Father's Day sermon, about earthly fathers modeling our heavenly One. After the service, we took him out to dinner at the Seven Gables. It was a nice, quaint restaurant with an expensive menu, but food that was worth the extra price. I sat beside Derek, and he got my whole family laughing with stories about his football coach. The stories weren't really that funny. But Derek told them in such a charming way that he delighted everyone.

He was not the most polished person, though. I found it

sweet when he didn't know which fork to use. I showed him in a discreet way by picking up my silverware first. He watched me like a hawk and imitated my every move. He never seemed embarrassed, but one time he was so excited about a story he was telling that he dropped his fork on the floor. He started to pick it up, and I bent down and whispered, "Leave it there." On the way back up, our foreheads bumped gently and we were close enough to kiss. It gave me a chill.

When I sat up, I saw Branson and his parents coming in the door. He was glaring and me and Derek.

I excused myself from the table and approached the Prices. After I wished Mr. Price a happy Father's Day, I kissed Branson on the cheek. He turned his head away.

"I missed you," I whispered.

"I'm having dinner with my parents," he said coldly. "We'll talk later."

I returned to my seat and enjoyed our Father's Day dinner.

When I got home I thought about Branson all evening. Dad opened the gift my brothers and I had pitched in for, but which I had picked out. He said he couldn't wait to wear his new suit to church the next Sunday.

When it was time to go to bed, I lay there looking up at the ceiling, praying my boyfriend and I could work things out between us.

Around two in the morning I heard a tap on my window. I opened it and found Branson standing there. During our junior year he used to sneak into my room whenever his parents got into one of their terrible arguments. He'd park his car down the road and walk almost a mile just to spend time talking with me.

"You look beautiful," he said when I let him in.

"What are you doing here?" I asked in a whisper, grabbing a robe to put on over my nightgown.

He took my robe and tossed it into the corner, then started taking off his shoes. The next thing I knew, he was on top of me in my bed, kissing me in a harsh way that offended me. I tried to get him to stop without making too much noise. As we rustled in the bed, my lamp clattered to the floor.

"Why don't you want this?" Branson asked, still straddling me. "You say you love me, but every time I see you, you're smiling at that black guy. If it was him kissing you, would you stop him?" Branson took off his shirt and then pinned my hands to the bed. When the hallway floor outside my door squeaked, my heart sank to my feet.

Part of me wanted someone to come in and stop Branson, but the other part didn't want to get caught. This could be the end for Branson and me. Then again, maybe it should be. I was so confused.

"Someone's coming," I hissed. But he didn't stop.

"Listen," he whispered, still on top of me. "I want this, OK? You're saying you don't have any feelings for that black guy. Well, then, prove it. Show me you love me. I want you now, Laurel."

I pushed him off me with every ounce of my strength. He tumbled off the side of the bed and onto the floor with a too-loud thud.

"This has nothing to do with Derek," I seethed as he rubbed his elbow. "You're the one I love, but this isn't right. If I did this, I wouldn't be honoring my Father."

sweating the temperature

b ranson!" Sweat moistened my upper lip as my bedroom door squeaked open. My boyfriend grabbed his shirt and scrambled behind the door.

"Laurel, honey, are you up?" my father asked, peeking in.

"Yeah, Dad. I'm having a hard time going to sleep."

"I heard some noises in here. Are you OK?"

"I'm fine." I started to pull up the covers when I noticed Branson's wallet on my bed. I shuffled my feet, flipping part of the blanket over the evidence.

I waited for my dad to leave the room, but he just stood there staring at me. It was like he could sense Branson behind the door. I pretended to yawn so I could wipe the perspiration off my upper lip as I covered my mouth.

"You should try to get some rest," he said. "It's 2:00 A.M."

"I know. I'm sorry I woke you up."

He stroked his chin as if he wasn't sure what to do next. "Truth is, I couldn't sleep either."

"Why not?" I clutched the edge of my comforter to stop my hands from trembling.

"I was just wondering how things are going to be for you in college. No rules. No parents. No curfew. Nobody watching. I hope your mom and I have instilled a high regard for moral integrity in you. If some two-bit chump comes by singing a nice song and doing a good dance, I wouldn't want you to fall for it."

All of a sudden I understood. My dad wasn't lingering because he suspected what was going on. He was going to miss me. He was having of those parent moments, realizing that his baby girl had grown up. Knowing that this was the last Father's Day I would be at home must have really hit him hard.

"You need to be able to stand for Christ when the intensity of peer pressure is applied," he said. "Will you succumb to it? Will you turn away from everything we taught you, all that you say you believe now?"

My dad was standing at my door in the middle of the night giving me a sermon. And my boyfriend was behind the door hearing every word. I sat in my bed sweating bullets because the very thing my father was talking about, the thing he was hoping I wouldn't do, was the exact position I was in. Sure, I'd told Branson no. But I needed to be stronger. I had to make sure Branson understood my convictions. I couldn't let him think I would give in to what he wanted. I felt like God had sent my dad into my room while I was being faced with tough issues to remind me that I knew better.

"I think I can go to sleep now, Dad," I said. "You can go back to bed."

He didn't ask any more questions. That was a good thing because I didn't want to tell him an untruth like, "Yeah, Dad. Don't worry about me. No one's ever going to pressure me into doing anything. You're going to be proud of me because I'm always going to be a good girl at Georgia.

Hey, I'm a good girl now. I don't have a boy in my room at two in the morning." Not that he would have asked all that, but I was thankful that he just turned around and walked out, closing the door gently behind him. As soon as the door shut, Branson fell to his knees.

"Shhh," I whispered. "My dad's got Superman ears."

"It's hot in here," Branson said quietly as he pulled the string on my antique ceiling fan.

"You've got to go," I said.

He grabbed his wallet, stuffed it back in his pocket, and sat on the edge of my bed. "Your dad's going to bed. He won't be back. Let's just enjoy each other for awhile."

I wanted to pound my knuckles on his head. "Earth to Branson. Didn't you hear what he just said?"

"Yeah." He chuckled. "The old man didn't even know I was in here."

"My father knows me really well. I'm sure he realized the things I've been thinking about our relationship."

He grinned. "So, what have you been thinking? Are you saying you want me?" He threw back the covers and cuddled up next to me, so close I could smell alcohol on his breath.

"You didn't tell me you were drinking," I said, pushing him away.

"I just had a rum and Coke and one joint. So what? I'm a bad boy. I like being bad." He grabbed the back of my neck.

As he started slobbering kisses all over my face, I kept hearing my dad's voice. He was right. I could do this. I didn't want to lose Branson, but I was tired of telling him no. It was painfully obvious that we weren't on the same page. His drinking and smoking pot and then inviting himself over to my bedroom in the wee hours of the morning really made me angry.

I hopped up. "You don't have any respect for me. You've completely ignored everything I've been saying. But the days of me accommodating your feelings are over. I am a high school graduate. My dad was right. I'm going to have to be responsible for my own decisions, as tough as they may be."

Branson blinked in confusion. "So, what are you saying?"

I stood straight, my shoulders back. "I'm telling you to leave. Now!" I could barely believe I'd just said those words.

"What do you mean?" He stood and grabbed my arm. "Laurel, you know what I came for and I want it now."

"Why are you doing this?" I asked, pulling away from his grasp. "Why do you have to push everything? I'm not ready yet. Can't you understand that? I love you, Branson, but you're crossing the line. I am not going to let you take advantage of my love and push me into doing something I'll regret. I'm tired of being weak around you. How dare you demand that I have sex with you? It's disgusting. You want to threaten me and say we're through? Fine. Get out and don't come back. Ever!"

I straightened my arm and pointed to the open window. A cool breeze blew in, making me realize how much all that tension and tears had made me sweat. My nightgown clung to my body. Branson leered at me, as if everything I had just said made no difference to him.

His eyes raked my curves even as I tried to cover myself with my arms. "The moonlight is hitting your body just right." He looked up into my eyes. "Oh, Laurel, I'm sorry. I know it seems like I'm pushing you, but you're so gorgeous."

He kissed my neck and then stopped when I stepped back. "Please don't be mad at me. I'm going through a lot right now. My dad's gone on one of his long business trips and my mom thinks he's cheating again. I just wanted to be with the one woman who cares about me. I guess I shouldn't have come."

Branson sank bank onto the bed. "I probably won't get the scholarship to Georgia after all. But I can't talk to my father about it because he'll just call me weak. He said I messed up any chance to make something of myself because I wasn't smart enough to get an academic scholarship. You know I'm not a bad student. Salem was hard and I was carrying a 2.9 GPA. But that wasn't good enough for him."

Branson started crying. I knew he was acting all emotional because he was drunk and high, but he did have some legitimate concerns. I took a step closer and he looked up at me. His gaze made me feel beautiful, but at the same time I knew it was sinful.

"I'm sorry you're going through so much." I put on my robe and handed Branson the glass of water on my nightstand.

"Thanks," he said, then took a long drink. "I'm OK now."

"Then I want you to go home," I said, quietly but firmly. "And please don't call me tomorrow."

He looked up at me with a sorrowful expression. "How are you going to know if I get home safe?"

"Just be careful. God will get you there."

"Am I worthless, Laurel?" he asked, looking up at me with those big puppy-dog eyes of his.

"No," I told him. "The world wouldn't be the same without you." I sat beside him on the bed and prayed for all the issues he was facing.

After I said, "Amen," he climbed back out of my window, blew kisses at me, and disappeared into the darkness. I couldn't believe, after everything that had just happened, that we were still a couple.

Please get him home safely, Lord, I prayed.

———————

I really wanted to stay home the next Saturday and chill with Brittany and Meagan. We didn't have many more nights together before they'd be leaving for Florida and I'd be headed off to Georgia. So I thought it would be nice to spend a quiet evening at my house reminiscing about the past and planning for the future.

Then Brittany found out about a rave party some kids from Kennesaw were having. I'd heard those parties were bad news, but Brittany said they were a lot of fun, and Meagan went along with her, so I was outvoted.

I could have said no. I should have said no. But I didn't. The moment I stepped into the abandoned warehouse, I wished I had.

The music was blasting. The dance floor was packed. Drugs and alcohol were everywhere. Kids were sprawled all over the place, most of them stoned. Guys had girls pushed into corners, and just a glimpse of what I saw nearly made me gag. It was worse than an R-rated movie.

"Let's get out of here," I said.

"No way," Brittany argued. "Relax. Mingle. Try to find somebody to dance with."

"Yeah," Meagan said, looking around with wide eyes.

I didn't want to argue with them, but I was extremely uncomfortable and I couldn't understand why they seemed so comfortable.

Why couldn't I stand up for what I wanted? Why did I have to give in to them every time?

There was nothing I could do about it now. Brittany drove and she wasn't leaving. Besides, I did have a lot to celebrate. Not the way a lot of these kids wanted to. But I was due for a good time.

"You want some punch?" Meagan asked me.

I remembered the New Year's Eve party at Brittany's house when I drank some spiked punch that made me buzzed and sick. My chest had burned and ached, and I felt like I was going to pass out.

"I'll pass on the punch," I told Meagan. "Think we could find some water, though?" Temperatures had reached over one hundred that day, and it hadn't cooled off a bit. The warehouse wasn't air conditioned, and all those bodies were making the air stifling.

A stranger stuck a bottle of Evian in front of my face. He was kind of cute, though not as clean-cut as I usually liked. He had greasy hair and a nose ring—definitely not my type.

"Were you eavesdropping on our conversation?" I asked.

"Just trying to be polite." He shrugged. "If you don't want it . . ." He started to tuck the bottle into one of the pockets in his baggy jeans.

"A gentleman would wait for my answer, not just take it back when I say something he doesn't like," I snapped back with a playful grin.

"Well, I'm not always a gentleman." He gave me a crooked half-smile. "If you want the water, it's yours. But if not, I'm gonna stand here and drink it in front of you."

His bad-boy attitude was kind of appealing. I checked to make sure the cap was sealed. Then I took the bottle, snapped off the cap, and gulped the water down.

"You were thirsty." The guy laughed.

I took another long drink and wiped my mouth with the back of my hand.

"It's not ladylike to guzzle," he said.

"Well, I'm not always a lady."

He smiled. "You wanna dance?"

Meagan nudged me toward him. "She'd love to."

I was glad it was a fast song. That put some distance between us.

Over the blare of the trance music, he asked me my name. I didn't respond right away. Then I figured it couldn't hurt. And I didn't want to be rude. He seemed like a nice guy. So I answered.

"Shadrach, huh? That's a weird name."

"What's yours?"

"Parc Reives. Parc with a *c*, not a *k*."

"That's weirder than Shadrach."

We laughed, and suddenly the music changed. Everyone around us started hugging up. Before I could think about it, I was dancing slowly in his arms. It didn't feel entirely comfortable, but it wasn't weird, either. Then I had a flash of my guy. What I was doing seemed wrong somehow. I backed away.

"You don't wanna dance anymore?"

"Sorry. I've got to go to the ladies' room. I'll talk to you later. It was nice meeting you." My palms were sweaty. It was a good thing my hair was pulled back in a ponytail because my temples were perspiring. Though I went from Dr. Jekyll to Miss Hyde on him, I didn't really care what he thought.

What is wrong with me? I wondered as I tried to find a quiet spot. That was hard to do because every inch of the room seemed occupied with someone doing something sinful. What did that say about me as a Christian? Surely God, my parents, and my boyfriend would all be unhappy with me in this environment.

"Boo!" Brittany said as she showed up behind me, Meagan beside her.

"You startled me."

"Don't be a whiner," Brittany said. "Meagan showed me that fine guy you were dancing with. Well, guess what? She and I have hooked up with his friends. They've got another party going on down the street where there's tons of food. Way more fun than this lame thing."

I did want something to eat, but another party? "I don't know," I said. "It's getting kind of late."

"We don't have to be home for two more hours," Meagan said.

"It's going to take forty-five minutes to get home."

"The party's close by," Brittany argued.

I knew they wouldn't let up, but I didn't really want to see that Parc guy again.

"Laurel, you never do what I want to do," Meagan whined. "I always go to your Bible studies. I always go to church with you. I always watch the movies you want to watch. For once, can't you just go where I want to go? This is supposed to be our farewell-to-high-school celebration. Don't be a party pooper. We won't stay long."

"Guess I don't have a choice," I said, squelching the tiny voice inside my head that said, *Yes, you do.* Instead I listened to the voice that said, *Let loose for a change. Have a good time. Be wild and enjoy yourself.*

When we got to the parking lot, I saw Parc and two other guys, who looked like members of a gothic rock band, standing beside a fiery red van with the side door open.

"What's going on?" I said.

"We're escorting you lovely ladies to the party," Parc said with that charming half-grin of his.

Brittany grabbed my arm and pushed me into the van. She and Meagan crawled in after me, followed by Parc's friends.

"I thought you were going to drive us to the party," I whispered to Brittany.

"They'll bring us back." She shoved me into the front passenger seat, then sat in the row behind me.

"We don't even know these guys," I said as Meagan settled into the back row. But it was too late. The van door banged shut. Parc flung himself into the driver's seat and the car started rolling.

The situation made me extremely nervous. But the air conditioning sure felt good.

Parc's weird-looking friends cuddled up with Brittany and Meagan, who clung to them like they were movie stars. Brittany introduced the guy she was with as Lex, and Meagan's partner as Streeter.

"You want some?" Lex asked, handing me a paper cup.

"No, thank you," I said. My throat was parched with thirst, but I wasn't about to drink something if I didn't know what it was.

I knew we were in trouble and I should pray for God to provide us with a way out. But I didn't feel right asking Him to help us since we'd been stupid enough to let ourselves get into this mess. So I sat there, planning to walk back to the rave party as soon as we got to the new one.

After about ten minutes I said, "I thought this party was right down the street."

"Calm down," Brittany said, her words slurred. She had obviously been drinking whatever was in that cup.

I looked back and saw Meagan kissing Streeter, totally ignoring everything else.

I glared at Parc. "Stop the car. Right now." When he didn't, I reached over to try to grasp the steering wheel.

"Hey, stop that," Lex hollered, grabbing my arm and yanking me to the middle seat.

"Don't push my friend around like that," Brittany said.

"You shut up," Lex ordered. Then he threw Brittany against me.

She glared at him. "And don't go shoving me around either."

Lex slapped her face with the back of his hand. She started crying in my arms.

"What's going on here?" I said. "Where are we going?"

"You want me to hush you up too?" Lex growled.

I was terrified. Images from news reports flashed through my mind. Who were these guys? Would we see tomorrow? Why was this happening?

I peeked into the backseat to check on Meagan. She was trying to stop kissing Streeter, but he kept pressing his lips to hers. She finally broke free and cried out, "You bit me!"

We were in serious trouble.

"Don't be scared, ladies," Streeter said.

"Let us go!" Brittany screamed. "This isn't fun anymore."

"Shut her up, man," Streeter warned.

Lex threatened Streeter with a shaking fist. "Don't push me."

"These guys are high," I whispered to Brittany. She nodded, her eyes wild with fear.

"Are they going to—" Before Meagan could finish her question, Streeter grabbed her hair and yanked it back.

"You know you want to give it to me. No one's gonna have to take anything. If you cooperate it'll be great."

He tried to kiss her, but she fought back.

"Don't fight it, babe," Streeter said.

"Just tell us where we're going," I said, trying to be rational with them.

"What difference is that gonna make?" Lex asked.

"I just want to know. Is it a secret?"

"We're not telling you anything," Lex barked, "so zip it." He crawled up into the front passenger seat to talk things over with Parc.

Brittany put her arm around me. "I've got a plan," she whispered.

"Don't do anything stupid," I whispered back.

"Well, I'm not going to just keep sitting here. Who knows what these guys are planning to do. We've got to get them back on our good side."

"Britt!"

She knelt between the driver's seat and the passenger seat, facing Lex, and started rubbing his chest and kissing his ear. Then she began unbuttoning his shirt.

"Yeah." He sighed. "I knew we chose the right girls."

"You can get all you want," Brittany said in a coy little voice. "I just don't want to feel like I'm being forced. Trust me, you'll like me much better if I freely give you what you want." She kissed him between every word. He seemed to be buying it.

"What can I do to make you feel more comfortable?" he asked.

"Let me go for now," she suggested. "I'll hook up with you tomorrow night. That way I can make it really special for you."

"Are you trying to get out of this?" he asked.

"Don't be crazy," Brittany said, her eyes twinkling with lustful promise.

The van came to a screeching halt. We stopped so suddenly Britt lost her balance and tumbled into the middle seat beside me.

Lex scrambled out and opened the side door. "We've got the goods," he bragged.

Outside the van stood twelve guys, their eyes hungry as if the three of us were their dinner. Streeter pushed us all out of the van, and we were enveloped in the hot, sticky night air. Then he got out behind us and shut the door.

When I saw Parc, I glared at him. But before I could speak, a large guy with bad acne grabbed my arm. "I'm going first." Another jerk gripped my other arm and said, "No, me." They pulled me like a wishbone, and their friends started doing the same thing with Meagan.

Before anyone could touch Britt, Lex said, "Back off. This one's mine." When she didn't follow him willingly, he grasped her hair and pulled her toward the upscale fraternity house across the lawn.

Suddenly our circumstances became crystal clear. These guys were college students. They had come to a high school party looking for underage girls. Meagan's crying started up again and I felt like joining her.

Parc came up to me as I struggled against the two guys. "Back off," he said. "She's with me."

"So you're not gonna share?"

Parc stepped closer and the other guys let go of me. He put his arm around me and steered me toward the frat house.

I struggled against him, but he kept pushing me. I let him have it with the only weapon I had: my mouth. I told him everything I hated about him until we got to the back of the house. Then he put his hand over my lips.

"Shhh," he said, letting go of my arm.

"What's going on here?" I screamed.

"I'm trying to figure out a way to get you and your friends out of this mess."

"But you were driving the car! Why did you bring us here in the first place?"

"I'm a freshman. I'm trying to make it into this fraternity and this is the initiation. I didn't think they were really going to do anything. I just thought we were going to have a little fun by scaring you girls and then taking you back."

I had no idea how we were going to get out of this. I thought about calling the police, but I figured by the time they arrived, these jerks would have time to do their damage to my friends.

I started doing what I should have done long before. I knelt right there in the grass and closed my eyes. "Heavenly Father, please forgive me. I know I've sinned. I shouldn't be where I am, but I'm here and I need Your help. I know there are always consequences when I do things outside of Your will. Lord, You're the only one who can help me out of this. And Meagan. And Brittany." Out of the blue, the Lord reminded me of what would happen if Brittany had sex with anyone. "Oh, my gosh," I blurted out. "If they . . . she could give them HIV!"

"What?" Parc cut in.

I looked up, embarrassed that he'd listened in on my private conversation with God. He dashed to the front of the house.

I followed quickly when I heard Meagan scream. "What are they doing to her?"

"You guys," Parc yelled, "we've got the wrong girls." He stood near the doorway of the frat house and announced, "They've got AIDS."

"What are you talking about?" Lex asked, bringing Brittany out from the side yard. Her clothes were dirty and ripped, but still on her body. Her face was flushed and streaked with tears, and her beautiful blond hair was a wreck.

"You're kidding, right?" He leered at Brittany. "She can't be infected. She's too pretty."

"Since when does outer beauty have anything to do with what's going on inside?" Brittany said. "You're fine-looking but you've been acting like a jerk ever since we left the rave party."

The rest of the gang came out of the house.

"Where's Meagan?" I yelled at them. She came running out the door with a bruised eye and a ripped blouse. She fell into my arms. As I held her I started blaming myself for this mess. I should have been witnessing to my friends. Though I felt like a nag sometimes, I didn't want to let them influence me into doing something that would lead us all into trouble.

"I think we'd better let them go," Parc told his friends.

Lex raised a fist at Brittany, but Parc held him back.

"How dare you?" Lex seethed at her. "You could have killed me."

"I wish we *had* done it," she lashed back. "'Cause you're the kind of guy I'd want to give this disease to."

Streeter grabbed Meagan, who was hiding behind me. "This little redhead is hot. She might be worth the risk. And I'll wear a condom."

Meagan pulled away and ran for the van. Brittany followed her.

"What should we do?" I asked Parc.

"Go on. I'll take you guys home."

As I followed my friends to the van, I heard Parc's fraternity brothers grumbling.

"Look, I'm out of here," he told them. "I'm not going to let you mess with these girls."

After I got into the van, my friends and I rolled up the windows and locked the doors. Then I turned around and saw Parc marching toward us.

"Let's beat 'em up," Lex hollered.

"Yeah!" Streeter said.

They all came charging at the van. Parc was in the lead, but I didn't know if he was going to make it to us before the other guys could pull us out and retaliate. I clutched Meagan's and Brittany's hands and squeezed.

It felt like over a hundred degrees in that van. But we weren't about to open any windows or doors.

Lex caught up to Parc and pushed him. Our rescuer fell face-first in the grass. The angry mob behind him advanced—angry, drunk, and enraged. They nearly trampled over Parc to get to us.

I was terrified of what they might do if they got into the van, but there was nothing I could do except watch as we sat there together, sweating the temperature.

popping
many fireworks

arc's going to help us," I assured Meagan and Brittany. "I just know it."

The three of us sat in the middle seat, our faces plastered to the side window of the van, watching the drunk, crazed guys running toward us.

"He's lying on the ground," Brittany shrieked. "There's nothing he can do."

The fraternity guys started pounding on the door, trying to break in to get us. My girlfriends and I pulled back, gathering in the middle of the backseat.

"Britt," I said, "do you have your cell phone?"

"Lex took it," she moaned.

"Mine's in the car at the rave," Meagan cried.

The van started rocking. "They're gonna turn this thing over," Brittany screamed.

"We've got to pray, you guys."

I wrapped one arm around each of my girlfriends. The

van was shaking, and we were trembling, and the heat made it difficult to breathe. "Lord, help us," I said.

Before I could say anything more, I heard what sounded like a splattering of small gunshots. We all screamed. But the rocking stopped.

"Someone's shooting at the van," Meagan squealed.

Brittany and Meagan clasped onto me. When I looked out the window, I saw Parc standing near the steps of the frat house. He carried two fistfuls of firecrackers.

"Check this out," I said, and the three of us stared out the side window of the van.

"What do you think you're doing?" Streeter snarled at Parc. "Why are you trying to help these girls leave?"

"Get over it, man," Parc said. "This is not what we set out to do tonight. I can't believe you guys used me to drive the car and didn't tell me what you planned on doing."

A guy yelled out from the crowd, "What you gonna do about it?"

"I've already called the cops. They can either drive by and see no disturbance, or you guys can keep acting crazy and go to jail. Now, get out of my way and let me drive these girls back to their car."

The guys moved away from the van and let Parc pass, like Moses through the Red Sea on dry land. I unlocked the driver's-side door. Parc hopped into the van, tossed the fireworks under the passenger seat, and drove off.

"Did you really call the police?" I asked, climbing up front with him. Then we passed a patrol car and I realized Parc was not bluffing. "Thank you," I said. "You probably ruined your chances with that fraternity. But you're a hero."

Parc snorted. "Those guys will probably respect me more and make me president of the fraternity. They're in desperate need of leadership. I've been following for a long time, not having the guts to tell them what they're doing is wrong. Tonight they pushed me too far. They weren't even thinking rationally. Drugs and beer will do that to you.

They're good guys, basically, but they do stupid things sometimes."

"Well, we're going to report them," Brittany said coldly.

We had every right to press charges, of course, but I could tell Parc was hoping his good deed would convince us not to. I tapped him on the shoulder and nodded to let him know I would talk to her, although I wasn't convinced that I didn't agree with her. I mean, if those guys got away without consequences, they would probably do this again to somebody else. I would feel terrible if we didn't create enough trouble to make somebody understand what these guys were doing before it was too late.

Meagan sat with her knees up against her chest, rocking back and forth, tears drenching her face.

"Meagan, what happened?" I asked tenderly.

She wouldn't say a word, just kept rocking.

"Did one of them do something?" I held my breath.

"Not all the way," Meagan said, her voice small and trembling. "Some of them touched me. But the stuff they said . . . that really got to me. They accused me of being loose because of my red hair. They kept saying, 'Everybody knows redheaded girls are easy.' "

"Yeah, and blonds are dumb bimbos," Brittany grumbled. "And brunettes are all serious and smart."

"Are you hearing yourself?" I chided her softly. "You're complaining about stereotypes based on hair color, but what about a person's skin?"

"I know," she said. "To be honest, I kinda like that girl Robyn. I guess I was just jealous that you wanted to hang out with her."

I climbed into the backseat and gave Brittany a long hug. Then I turned to Meagan. She released her knees and embraced both of us.

"That must be your car," Parc said as he rolled into the otherwise empty parking lot.

I looked at my watch. "Oh, no," I groaned. "It's four-thirty!" My parents were going to have a fit.

Brittany screamed. I followed her gaze out the side window and looked at her black Jetta. The back windows were all busted and every tire had been slashed.

"What are we gonna do?" Brittany moaned.

"How are we going to get home?" Meagan cried.

We found Meagan's cell phone in the glove compartment and I called home.

An hour and a half later, at six o'clock in the morning, my dad's burgundy Cadillac Seville pulled into the parking lot, followed by a tow truck. Parc left as soon as he saw that we were going to be all right.

Dad drove us home and the tow truck followed with Brittany's busted Jetta. As we rode home, I thought about the lessons we'd all learned that night.

Parc had stood up to his friends and done something courageous. Meagan learned she shouldn't flirt so much. Brittany realized she shouldn't judge others. And I discovered that there are some times when you've got to stand up to your friends.

My dad didn't say much to us, but I knew I was going to be in for it when we got home. And yet, somehow, that was OK. I wanted him to re-emphasize what I already knew. I had to be prepared for the worst because only time would tell what angry firecrackers would pop off next.

I figured we were in enough trouble, why lie about it? When we got to my house, Mom had biscuits and gravy waiting for us. I could smell it the moment we walked through the door. Then I saw Brittany's dad and Meagan's mom sitting at the table, and my appetite disappeared.

"You girls could have been killed," Brittany's dad said. "Why didn't one of you stand up to those jerks?"

Meagan's mom was crying too hard to say anything.

We all sat in my living room, and we were all feeling really bad.

Finally, Mrs. Munson collected herself enough to say, "The thought of you girls being—I can't even say it. What were you thinking, getting into a strange man's car?"

"Did you have to tell them everything?" Brittany mumbled to me.

My mother hugged us, served us breakfast, and brought us cool cloths so we could wash up.

"You girls didn't deserve anything that happened," my dad said, "but you did set yourselves up to be victimized."

"Your first mistake was going to that rave party," Mom added.

"We know what we did wrong," I said. "And we're sorry. We're not asking for you to forgive us." I felt Brittany kick my leg under the table. "Though it would be nice," I said, responding to her thump. "We have learned our lesson."

Brittany's dad stood and hugged her, really tightly. From her surprised response, I gathered he hadn't done that in a while. "I'd go crazy if I lost you."

Then Meagan got up and went over to her mom. "I was so scared."

"I called your father," Mrs. Munson said. "He was worried about you—ready to cut his business trip short—until I assured him you were safe."

I watched my friends get hugs from their parents. But my dad didn't hug me. Because he was a pastor, most people assumed he was a pushover, but he was a really tough guy.

After my friends left with their folks, my dad just stared at me, not saying a word. I kind of wanted to ask about my fate, but I didn't want to push the issue. I knew he was angry at me in spite of my little spiel about learning my lesson. I wanted to make him proud of me, but it was hard balancing right and wrong. In my mind there was a skewed gray line between the two.

Finally, I just thanked my parents again for their under-standing and quietly went upstairs, where I fell to my knees.

"Lord," I said, "I know I let my dad down. I let You down too. Thank You for coming to my rescue. I want to do better but I don't always know how to go about that. Please lead my thoughts. Guide me. In a way it doesn't seem right that we made it through that. But You spared us. You have so much patience and grace. Teach me how to take life one step at a time and make You proud. I know there's some-thing You want me to do with my life because You spared it. I'm going to make both You and my dad proud of me."

After I said "amen," I heard my mom's voice. I stood up and saw her standing in my doorway.

"Laurel, I want to talk to you about this destructive path you're on."

I climbed onto my bed, but she remained just inside the doorway, her arms crossed. I mentally prepared myself for the tongue-lashing I knew I deserved. "I'm sorry, Mom. I re-ally am."

"Laurel, your actions last night were despicable. And I take some responsibility for that."

What in the world was she talking about? She didn't make me go to the party. She didn't make me get into that van with those crazy guys. She wasn't responsible for my decisions.

She sat in the chair beside my bed. "You did something a few days ago that disturbed me, and I've been praying for you, but I haven't really known how to address it. I haven't even talked to your father about it."

I wrapped my arms around my knees and stared at her. "What are you talking about?"

"A few nights ago your father heard some noises in your room."

She didn't have to say any more. I knew this conversa-tion was leading to a big explosion.

"Your dad said you were just trying to get to sleep, but I

know what a sound sleeper you are. So when he went back to bed, I decided to come and pray for you. Before I could open the door, I heard a male voice. At first I thought it was one of your brothers, but when I listened more closely, I knew it was Branson. I just stood there, frozen. My baby girl was in her room with her boyfriend at three in the morning."

"I didn't have sex with him," I cut in.

"I heard you tell him he needed to leave. But Laurel, you know what he wanted. And for him to feel like he could come here at that hour implies that you're very close to doing it."

I couldn't be angry. It was time I talked to somebody. I needed to let all this out.

"OK, Mom. Do you want me to be honest with you? It's hard for me to be perfect. I'm not saying I'm ready to have sex, but part of me does want to. I didn't want to go to that party last night, but the excitement of celebrating graduation enticed me. If I could go back and do it all over again, I sure wouldn't have chosen what I did."

"You've got to be smarter in your choices. Your dad and I talked about punishing you and we've decided there's no point to it. You're almost out the door, and punishment might only make you act crazier when you get to Georgia. So we're going to give you a little room."

"Mom, I hate that I'm battling this stuff. I wish I could make you and Dad proud, but there's a battle inside me. Do you understand what I'm talking about? I'm sure you don't because you're the perfect homemaker mom."

"Oh, darling, I'm not perfect. None of us is. I've been where you are now, and my life is a lot different now because I changed some of the things I was doing. I stopped hanging around things that were tempting me."

"So are you telling me I should stop dating Branson?"

"No, honey. I'm not going to tell you what to do. I'm just saying you need to think about your decisions. If you know you'll be tempted by Branson, why go out with him? If he's pressuring you into doing things you don't want to do, maybe he's not the right guy for you. And if your girlfriends are encouraging you to do crazy things that are sinful and dangerous, maybe you need to think about what kind of friends you're hanging around with."

"Are you saying I shouldn't be with the people I care about?"

"I'm saying you should think about it. You need to decide things for yourself. If you want better results, you've got to change what you're doing. You know, there's nothing wrong with someone calling you a bore because you want to study the Bible instead of go to a party. It's OK to be a virgin. Being sober and sane is a lot safer than being drunk and crazy. There's got to come a point when you stand up for what you know is right, regardless of what others think." She touched my cheek. "Be the daughter I raised you to be. Be strong and follow God. If you do that, you'll be proud of every decision you make."

She kissed me on the forehead and left me to think about all that she'd said. I appreciated her being my friend as well as my mom. She was right. My life was in my own hands. What I did from this point on would determine my future. I needed to please God. And that meant sometimes I had to say no.

I got back on my knees and vowed to the Lord that if He would lead, I would follow. It seemed so easy to promise. As soon as I got off my knees, I wondered if I could really do it.

"Laurel, I need to see you tonight," Branson pleaded with me over the phone. "You haven't called me all week. I've got some big plans for tonight to celebrate the Fourth of July and your birthday."

I couldn't respond to him. It was like I had put myself on restriction. Meagan was grounded but Brittany was free to do whatever she wanted. For the first week after the party, my friends called me every day, begging me to do something with them. I said no to everything, without even asking my parents for permission. If no one was going to punish me, I was going to punish myself. Finally I'd told my brothers and Derek to take messages if any of my friends called.

That morning I was home by myself when the phone rang, so I'd picked it up.

"Do you want me to ask your mom if you can go?" Branson asked.

"No!" I almost screamed. *"You're not one of her favorite people right now."* I let a silent pause happen, then said, "OK. We can get together. Pick me up around eight."

That afternoon my mom made a great meal for lunch and my family all gave me presents—all except Lance. I had told him not to buy me anything until he paid off his debts. He made me a birthday card, though, from construction paper and glitter and different-colored pens. He even wrote a poem on the card. It wasn't fancy and it didn't really rhyme, but I could tell it came from his heart, and that made it special.

As I helped Mom wash the lunch dishes, I told her about my plans to go out with Branson that night.

"So you've already committed to going out with him without asking your father or me?" she asked in an edgy voice.

"You said I wasn't going to be punished," I reminded her.

"You could have at least checked with us first. It is your birthday, you know."

"And I really appreciate the great lunch you made for me and all the presents," I said. "I didn't realize you'd want more of my time tonight."

I was so confused. As I looked into my mom's eyes, I could tell she was too. I knew she was happy I'd chosen to stay in all week. And that I'd been spending so much time reading the Bible and Christian books. The only places I'd gone since that horrible party were church, Mrs. Meaks's discipleship group, and practice at Rockdale County Gym.

"Mom, I really have learned a lot this week. I thought about what you told me. I can't make any promises that I won't do anything stupid, but I can tell you that the likelihood of that happening is small. Branson is not going to cross any lines with me. I do love him, and I want to be there for him. But I'm not going to sleep with him. That simply won't happen. You don't have to worry."

"So where are you guys going?" she asked.

I hated to say I didn't know, but I didn't want to make up something. "He said it was a surprise."

Mom raised her eyebrows at me.

"I can get more details, or at least tell him to communicate with you and dad so you'll know where we're going."

Just then Lance walked into the kitchen. "You guys talking about tonight?" he asked, grabbing an apple from the fridge. "I heard there's a big fireworks party out at the Horse Park. Bo's going to be there."

"Really?" I asked. "When did he get out of the hospital?"

"Yesterday. He's in a wheelchair, but he's still planning to celebrate."

Was that Branson's surprise? If so, why didn't he tell me?

"Are you going?" I asked my brother.

"Yeah, I was planning to."

"You both need to be in by 11:30," Mom said.

That was a half-hour before my normal curfew. So I figured I was getting some punishment after all. I thought she was pulling my chain in a little early, but I could live with that.

Branson picked me up at six. "You're two hours early," I complained. "It's still light out. What are we going to do till nine?"

"You'll see."

I let him drive and was surprised when he took me to

121

the scene of the prom-night accident. When he pulled into the Evergreen Hotel parking lot, I said, "I'm not getting a room with you."

"Don't worry. We're not going in. I just wanted to come back here, and you were the only person I could think of that I'd want to go through all this with."

I didn't know what to say to him. This was a serious side of him I'd never seen.

"I wish what happened to Bo had happened to me instead," he said, his voice breaking. "I'm the one who talked him into entering the race."

I felt sorry for Branson when I saw him shed some tears. He was being so transparent that I could see his pain.

"The football team is going to honor Bo at the fireworks show. It'll be the first time I've seen him since . . . that night." He looked out the window at the cliff Bo's car had gone over. "Tonight we're going to see each other face to face, and I don't know how he's going to feel about that."

I wiped his tears with my thumb and stroked his cheek. "You know, there are lots of actions I wish I could take back."

"Yeah, right," he scoffed. "You're Little Miss Perfect."

"Trust me, I'm not," I said, unable to look at him.

When he refused to believe me, I told him about the events of the previous weekend.

"You did what?" he said over and over as I related the details.

"What I'm trying to tell you is that everybody does stupid things they wish they could take back."

"OK, you did something stupid. But the consequences could have been much worse. Bo will never walk again, but I'm all healed. It doesn't seem right. I don't know how I'm going to live with myself."

I held him in my arms for a long moment, asking God for the right words to say to him.

"You know, we can't be made whole on our own. We need a Savior."

"Don't talk to me about God right now." Branson opened his glove compartment and pulled out an unopened envelope, which he handed to me. It was from the doctor's office. "The results of my last AIDS test." He looked down. "I can't open it. I need you to tell me my fate."

"Do you want to pray first?"

He didn't respond, so I started in. "Lord, it's hard for my boyfriend to trust You right now. So I ask that You will come into his heart, forgive him of his sins, and show him grace. We all make mistakes. Lord, if the results are not what we want, I ask You to give us the strength to deal with that. Amen."

When I opened my eyes I saw Branson staring at me. "Why would you say that?"

"I don't know what the results are. God doesn't always do what we want, particularly when we don't really know Him. But He loves you, and He wants to be there for you."

"Forget it." He snatched the envelope out of my hand. "If I'm gonna die, I might as well know it."

He stared at the envelope.

"It could work out," I said.

"I'm scared, Laurel." He grasped my hand. "I honestly don't believe I'm going to have any reason to be popping many fireworks."

e L e v e N

trying
to change

branson pounded his fists on the steering wheel, saying all kinds of nasty words. Then he buried his face in his hands.

"Branson, I know right now you feel—"

"You don't know what I'm feeling. You're not holding an envelope with your fate in it."

I could have snapped back, but I realized he wasn't thinking clearly. At that moment he needed grace. "You're right, I don't know how it feels to be in your place. But I do care that you're going through all this. And whatever happens, I love you. Nothing is going to change that. It's going to be OK."

He handed me the envelope. I kissed his forehead. In the last bit of daylight, I opened the envelope and read the letter inside.

"Branson, you're OK! Your tests were negative!"

He sat there staring at me, unable to process my words.

"Let me read it to you." I cleared my throat. "Dear Mr. Price. I am pleased to inform you that the results of your HIV tests are negative. I recommend you come in for annual retests over the next three years. Feel free to contact me if you have any questions or concerns, or if you experience any of the symptoms we discussed. Sincerely, Dr. Drake Dickinson."

Branson leaned over the center console and put his arms around me, pulling me toward him. "Thanks for being there for me. I love you, Laurel." He kissed me, and I felt the passion of the moment, so I quickly pulled away. "We'd better get going. Don't want to miss the fireworks show."

"Yeah," he said. "We really do have something to celebrate!"

Along the way, I tried to convince him it was God who'd worked the miracle for him, but he just called it good luck. Still, I knew God was doing something great with Branson. He was knocking at the door of his heart, which was what I'd been praying for. Next on the Lord's agenda was breaking my guy to a point where he would realize he needed God. I wasn't wishing anything bad on Branson, but I knew the Lord operated that way sometimes.

My actions needed to speak louder than my words. It was one thing to say, "Try God," but he needed to see that I had peace because I believed in Someone greater than myself or anyone in this world. I hadn't always shown godly character with Branson, but I was determined to change that.

When we walked into the park, I saw Bo in his wheelchair.

"Hey, guy," Branson said, his voice stuttering and hands trembling. "It's . . . It's good to see you, man."

To help my boyfriend regain his dignity, I knelt beside the wheelchair and said, "It really is good to see you, Bo." I placed my hand on his. "I've been praying for you."

I didn't know why I said that. Bo had always hated God,

but the words were out of my mouth before I thought about how he'd take them.

Bo looked me in the eye. "I've been feeling your prayers."

My eyes misted, and I noticed his did too. I wrapped my arm around his shoulder and gave him a sisterly hug.

He looked up at Branson. "Don't be nervous, man," he said with a smile. "I can't even move. Your girlfriend's safe with me."

We walked around the park together, and several people came up to ask how Bo was doing and wish him well. Even some of the really popular kids chatted with him.

The guys from the football team started cheering, "Rah, rah, Bo! Rah, rah Bo!"

Branson grumbled and walked away from the crowd.

"We'll be back," I whispered to Bo.

"I want to talk to him, Laurel. I need him to know I'm OK. I've got something better now than I had before. I've got Christ."

That melted my heart like a chocolate morsel on a hot sidewalk.

I walked beside Bo as he drove his electric wheelchair up to Branson. "Somebody wants to talk to you," I said to his back.

He turned around, his eyes bright with unshed tears. "I'm sorry, man."

"Me too." Bo said.

"Seeing you like this, it . . . it just makes me mad."

"I was angry too," Bo said. "But I had nowhere to direct my anger. I couldn't be mad at God, because I didn't believe in Him."

"You *didn't* believe?" Branson asked. "What are you saying?"

"A good friend of mine helped me get my life back together. He helped me see that God wanted me to give my anger to Him. Even though I'll never walk again, there's still something God wants me to do."

It was great hearing Bo talk this way. He'd found God in the midst of his tragedy!

"Physically, I don't have much anymore. But I have everything because I have Christ."

"But you'll never walk again." Branson's voice cracked.

Bo shrugged. "Miracles do happen," he said. "The Lord can heal me, if He chooses to. Or He may do even greater things in my life."

Branson dug his toe into the ground. "You didn't call me when you got out of the hospital," he said in a sulking voice.

"I'm sorry about that," Bo said. "I didn't want anyone around when I first got home. Now I'm ready for my friends again, but I have new conditions. For one thing, don't pity me. And don't blame yourself. I want friends who will lift me up, not help me stay down. But the biggest condition is this: You have to be open to hearing about God. I need friends who won't push me into sin."

Branson stared at the ground. "That's a lot to think about," he mumbled.

"Take your time," Bo said. He pushed the button on his wheelchair and drove off.

"He's a different guy, Laurel," Branson said, not at all happy about the transformation.

"He's a better guy," I said. Before we could discuss it further, fireworks started going off in the sky.

———————————

A week later, I woke up feeling great. It occurred to me that my ankle hadn't bothered me in quite awhile, and I thanked the Lord for that.

Branson called to tell me he'd taken a job at Six Flags. He'd have long hours during the summer, he said, so he wouldn't be able to call me all the time. I knew part of me would miss him, but another part looked forward to having some space so I could think things through.

I couldn't get Bo off my mind. I kept replaying his testimony in my mind. Throughout the four years I'd known him, he was a thorn in my side. Every time I brought up Jesus, he said I was crazy. Now that he would never walk again, he was happier than I'd ever seen him.

I wanted that fire. Though I didn't like admitting it, it was clear that my relationship with God wasn't as strong as Bo's. But how could I get there?

I had an idea. Before I could lose my nerve, I picked up the phone and called Bo.

That afternoon, I was sitting with Bo in his kitchen, eating a sandwich his mom had made. I acted like a reporter, asking tons of questions.

"You were always talking about God," he said to me. "So was my mom, and a lot of other people. I never thought I'd be encouraging someone to take their walk with God up a notch. But here I am, in a wheelchair the doctors tell me I'll never get out of. I believe God's got me here so that, for the rest of my days, I can tell people about Him."

"When did this change start?" I asked.

"The night I regained consciousness in the hospital, I was extremely bitter. But two days later, I had an encounter with God, just like Paul on the road to Damascus. For some unknown reason, I fell out of the hospital bed and I couldn't get up. As I lay there on the floor, God spoke to me."

"What did He say?"

Bo's voice grew soft and reverent as he quoted the Holy Spirit's words. "If you want to get up, I will help you, but you have to let Me in. You can't get up alone. You need Me."

I stared at Bo in stunned amazement. Not only was his story incredible, but I was impressed that Bo knew about Paul in the New Testament. He must have been reading the Bible a lot since his transformation began.

"I don't know how much time went by. It felt like I lived the whole eighteen years of my life all over again. I thought about everything I'd done, why I did what I did, and the consequences of my actions. I finally realized that I really did need to let God into my life. I wanted to get up. I wanted to move on. I wanted a change. So I said, 'OK, God, if You're there, help me.' At that exact moment, my doctor came in. He helped me back into bed, but I couldn't stop crying. I knew God had answered my prayer, so I had to give Him my life."

"But you still can't walk, and you might never," I whispered.

"That's true," he said without flinching. "But I have a new Christian walk now, and I'm stepping higher than I ever did on two feet."

I couldn't believe how happy he seemed. "Don't you want to walk again?"

He laughed. "Of course."

"Do you think you will?"

"I don't know," he said matter-of-factly. "If the Lord wants me to, I will. But I'm not focusing on what I don't have. I'm focusing only on Him."

I took a deep breath, wondering if I would have that kind of faith if I were in his situation. I had a hard time focusing on the Lord when far less dramatic things happened in my life.

"I'm sorry I was such a jerk toward you," he said. "I probably tarnished your walk with Christ. Maybe that's why God has me telling you now that you can make your relationship with Him stronger."

Things were starting to feel uncomfortable, so I changed the subject to get the focus off of me. "Have you told Branson about all this?"

Bo looked down. "He hasn't called me once since I gave him the new parameters for our friendship."

"How do you feel about that?" I knew how I'd feel if I set those parameters and then Branson never called me.

"I'm hurt, sure. And disappointed. But I'm not broken. God is mending my heart. He's changed it. The things that were important to me aren't that big a deal anymore."

"So, how do I get what you have?" I asked.

Bo looked at me, confused. "What are you talking about? You already know the Lord."

"I accepted Christ as a little girl. I've always been a Christian. But my relationship with Him is like . . . well, like marriage can get when two people have been together for a really long time. I'm not as excited about Him as you are. The fire has died down. Can you help me?"

Bo smiled at me. "You're off to a good start just by asking that question."

"So, what's the answer?" I persisted.

"I guess I'd have to say that you need to look at your life and let go of some of the baggage that's pulling you into sin."

"But what if it's your best friend or your boyfriend that's pulling you down?" I asked.

"You know, I always wanted Brittany to be my girl," Bo said.

"Really?" I asked, completely shocked.

"I secretly longed for her all through high school, and I was really angry when she chose Branson over me. Then Branson had to get an AIDS test because of her. And I realized that although she *looked* good to me, she wasn't. I still love her, and I know God wants me to remain friends with her. Jesus walked among sinners to change them, but He didn't become like them."

"You sure know a lot about God for someone who just became a Christian," I remarked.

Bo smiled. "I've been spending a lot of time reading His Word. And I'm in a Christian chat room with some really strong believers. You should check it out."

"Maybe I will." I determined right then that I was going to be more like Bo. Considering what this guy had been like for most of the time I'd known him, the thought seemed pretty ironic.

When I went to church the next day, Mrs. Meaks confirmed what Bo had told me.

"Equally yoked," she told our Sunday school class, "is not just about Christians marrying believers. It's about living as believers in everything we do. When the sun rises, darkness disappears. The two don't mix. So, which are you, light or darkness? Whichever you choose, let your life reflect your choice."

My thoughts immediately connected Mrs. Meaks's words with Bo's advice. But my thoughts were jarred when I heard her say, "Yes, Foster?"

My eyes followed her gaze. There sat my ex-boyfriend, whom I hadn't seen since school let out.

"I had to make tough choices," he said, "and let go of someone who was dear to me." It didn't take a genius to figure out he was talking about me. I wondered how many other people in the room figured it out. "She wanted me to be different from what God called me to be."

He looked right at me, and I couldn't look away. He was telling me what was on his heart, and God knew I needed to hear his words.

Foster turned his attention to the rest of the class. "I just want to say something to those of you who are hanging around someone because you want to lead them to Christ or help them live a godly life, but it's not working. If that person is pulling you away from your walk with Christ, you need to cut the cord. It won't be easy."

He took a deep breath. "As most of you know, I'm a recovering alcoholic. I didn't want to let go of booze. But the Lord gave me the strength to be made whole again. Now I take things one day at a time. In the same way, my love for this other person didn't leave when we went our separate ways, even though I've prayed for that every day. But I'm not bitter. God is mending my heart. And He's teaching me that life is not about finding another person to be with. It's about keeping a strong relationship with the Lord."

"Thank you for sharing that," Mrs. Meaks said.

I wasn't falling for Foster again, but I felt bad that when he needed me to love him I couldn't. So after class I walked up to him and said, "I want you to know I get what you're saying now. Thanks for reminding me that if I walk with God I'll be OK."

"I'm glad to hear that," he said, his brown eyes sparkling.

"I'm sorry I made you feel like you did," I added, "especially when you were recovering from alcohol."

Foster chuckled. "For weeks I called myself a recovering Laurel-holic."

I laughed with him. It felt great to be friends with him again.

"Seriously, Laurel, I haven't stopped praying for you. It's not easy choosing God over someone you love who's pulling you away from Christ. But I can honestly say I have recovered from both alcohol and you. And if God can change me, He can change you too. But you've got to completely choose Him."

He gave me a lot to think about.

Branson wasn't at church that day, which bothered me. I knew he had to work weekends, but surely he could have scheduled his hours around church. God just wasn't a priority for him. I didn't know if I was a priority, either.

My dad gave an awesome sermon that day. He talked about being a branch connected to the vine. If you're not connected, he explained, you can't bear fruit. But Christians who are connected to God can bear fruit for His kingdom. Branches grow fruit because they're connected to the vine, not because they're connected to the dirt that surrounds them. Branches that are on the ground will never bear fruit. But the ones that stay on the tree will survive through harsh winters, and in the springtime they'll blossom again. God can use our down times for His glory.

My dad's message reinforced what I'd been learning that week. In order to grow closer to God, I had to grow away from some of my friends. It wasn't a choice I wanted to make, but I knew I had to.

Suddenly I felt like running up and down the aisle. I could do this! I was going to make the change.

After church Meagan came up to me and asked how I was doing. About twenty times in a row I said, "I'm doing great. God is so good." I sounded like a Holy Roller! I was high in the Spirit.

———————————

· Later that night I was sitting on the porch with my dad. He was reading his Bible, but kept glancing up at me. I was so full of passion for Christ I must have been bouncing the porch swing.

"Your ankle must be feeling better today," he said.

Oh, yeah, my ankle was fine. But that wasn't the source of my joy. I wanted to tell him why I was so happy. But I was a little scared. After putting in hours of service to God, preaching, teaching, counseling, and praying, my dad was still studying the Word. Could I be that committed? Would my new fire last?

"What's on your mind?" he asked, closing his Bible.

"I'm just really happy because I feel the Holy Spirit," I said.

He looked at me with a surprised expression.

"But I'm also scared because I don't know if I'll have this same joy tomorrow. I've felt like this before, but the fire always cooled. I want to feel this excited about God all the time. I'm so full of thinking about Him. I'm no longer worried or nervous about college or my future or any of that. I feel perfectly safe about everything."

I stood and walked to the edge of the porch. "When I hold your hand, I can feel how much you care about me. Well, I can feel in my heart right now that God is close to me. I want to stay that way, but I'm afraid I don't know how."

My father joined me at the porch railing and wrapped his arms around me from behind. He prayed in my ear, practically blowing blessings all over my life. I felt like my heavenly Father was showing me His plan. And all I had to do was talk to Him about the tough stuff, and He would guide me through it.

My dad turned me around. "One step at a time, Laurel. That's how you'll stay fired up." He took my hands in his. "Yield every step to Him. Give every decision to Him, every thought to Him, every friend to Him. What He does with your life will be better than anything you could ever do." He brushed back a lock of hair the wind had blown out of place. "I've been parenting you for eighteen years. Now I give you back to God. I can see that He's shining His mercy and grace on you. He's shown me that He's really got your heart. So be committed to change your life in whatever ways are necessary to glorify Him. Don't just be trying to change."

ending
the romance

S o, where we going?" I asked my boyfriend in the car. "I have tons of plans to make our anniversary fabulous."

Branson and I had been off and on for three and a half years. We started dating the summer before our sophomore year, when I saw him at a country club where he was the lifeguard. I'd liked him since the ninth grade, but he always hung with the popular crowd. I remembered the first thing he said to me: "You're that girl at my school. You look incredible."

I had on a bathing suit, and at that moment I knew I had him hooked. Our relationship hadn't always been fun, but I'd always loved him. And when he remembered the anniversary of our first date, it melted my heart.

I took a long sniff of the fresh bouquet of flowers he'd given me moments earlier. "The suspense is killing me, Branson. Where are we going?"

"OK, if you can't hold on for the surprise, I'll tell you. We're going to my house."

A lump formed in my throat. My body started shaking.

"My mom fixed a nice meal for us. My parents said this night should be special for us, and they wanted to help us celebrate it."

"Oh," I said, greatly relieved. "Sounds great."

When he pulled up to his house I saw a dim light in one room, but otherwise the place was dark.

"My parents are big romantics," he explained. When he opened the front door I saw candles lit in the dining room.

"It's so pretty," I said.

He closed the door behind us and kissed my neck. "Not as pretty as you."

"Mrs. Price, we're here," I called out, heading for the kitchen. "What smells so good?" My voice seemed to echo through the house.

I entered the dining room and found the table beautifully decorated. But my doubts multiplied when I saw that the table was only set for two. Branson invited me to sit, but I didn't.

"What's going on here? This is unacceptable. You know I'm not—"

"Calm down," he said.

"Where are your parents? You told me they wanted to help us celebrate."

"Yes. They made it possible for us to have a quiet, romantic evening alone."

"This isn't funny," I said, standing my ground.

"Laurel," he said softly, looking deeply disappointed, "my mom made us a delicious dinner. Then she and Dad made themselves scarce for a few hours so we could enjoy it. They're fine with this."

"Well, my parents wouldn't approve."

"Lighten up, Laurel." he said. "It's our anniversary. Let me show you how glad I am that we've made it through all that we have. I love you and I'm just trying to do something nice."

His eyes looked so forlorn, I didn't have the heart to argue anymore. He pulled out one of the chairs, and I sat. He sniffed my hair as he helped me push in the chair, then he sat beside me .

Branson picked up a jumbo chilled shrimp and popped it into my mouth. It tasted divine. After I ate six more of them, he took the plate to the kitchen and brought back two Caesar salads. The main course was stuffed flounder with asparagus and a big baked potato. Branson poured a delicious carbonated punch from a crystal pitcher into matching goblets.

"Your mom didn't have to go all out like this," I said. "But I'm sure glad she did. This is all so yummy!"

When I couldn't eat another bite, Branson said, "Ready for dessert?"

I raised my eyebrows as he slipped back out to the kitchen.

I sat there wondering what delicious pastry his mom had prepared, and if I could find room in my stomach for it. But when Branson returned, he was carrying an adorably wrapped package with the words *Happy Birthday* on it. I laughed.

"I'm sorry this is so late," he said. "But I got my letter from the doctor on your birthday, and I was really worried about what it said. I was also concerned about seeing Bo at the fireworks show that night. I wasn't even sure what our status was as a couple, since you hadn't called me in awhile. So I figured I'd wait a while and give this to you when I knew we were OK."

"Better late than never," I teased.

"I have an anniversary gift for you too." He handed me a smaller box, also cutely wrapped. "Open this one first."

When I pulled off the beautiful paper, I was delighted to see a picture of the two of us in a wooden frame. We were on our first date at the Atlanta Zoo, with Lumani and Yon Yon, two baby pandas, in the background.

"I love this," I said. I felt my resistance melting. But I had no intentions of giving in. I stood to give Branson a great big hug, but as soon as I did, I felt light headed.

"I'm a little woozy," I said, sitting back down.

"Then you'd better not drink any more of this." He took my almost-empty punch glass to the kitchen.

"What do you mean? Branson, did you put alcohol in this punch?"

"No," he said, returning with a glass of water. "Just Champagne. You know, a little something to celebrate with."

I was miffed at his false pretenses. How dare he try to get me drunk!

Before I could get too upset, he put the other box in my hand. "Don't forget this one."

The box was pretty and I didn't want to ruin the moment, so I opened it. Inside was a cream-colored silk G-string from Victoria's Secret. I was stunned.

"Why don't you go try it on?" he suggested.

I threw the box at him. Then I started hitting him with my fists.

"What are you doing?" he yelled, defending himself from my blows.

"Why did you have to ruin everything?" I hollered. "I don't want to have sex with you. Why do you have to keep pushing me?"

He shoved me off him so hard I knocked my dinner plate into the centerpiece candle, which fell over, spilling hot wax all over the tablecloth.

I had intended to help Branson wash the dishes, but now all I wanted to do was go home. I grabbed my purse, but left the gifts on the table. I insisted that Branson take me home immediately, and I didn't say another word to him the whole way. I didn't even let him walk me to the door.

"Why are you still in bed?" Brittany asked as she came into my room two days later.

"Britt, I told my brothers I didn't want any company. You never listen. You always think everything is about you."

"I'm not alone. Come on in, girl." She ducked outside my door and pulled Robyn in.

I didn't want to admit to them that my boyfriend and I were having serious problems again. But I hated not being transparent with them. After all, these were my closest friends. If I couldn't share with them what was going on with me, what kind of friendship did we have?

Branson hadn't phoned me since our anniversary incident. I called him to make sure he was OK and that his mother wasn't upset about her ruined tablecloth. But the answering machine was the only thing that heard my concern. I left messages on his cell phone and his voice mail, but he didn't call me back. That meant only one thing: a breakup was inevitable. I didn't want to break up with him, but then, I kinda did, because his lack of values had compromised my integrity too many times. I sure didn't want to crawl back to him. I had to stand and be unwavering in my beliefs.

"So, what's going on with you and Branson?" Brittany asked, making herself comfortable on the edge of my bed.

"Let's not talk about me. Why did you come over here?"

"Laurel, dang!" Robyn said in her cute ghetto way.

Hanging around her had taught me a lot. At first I thought the reason black people "broke English" was because that was all they knew. After getting close to Robyn, I learned that the things they said, and the way they said them—with a roll of the eyes and a twist of the neck—usually make a pretty powerful point. And Robyn's talk often made me laugh.

"I'm glad I could make you crack a smile," she said.

"Thanks, you guys, but I'm OK. What's going on with you two?"

Robyn sat on the chair by my bed. "We got this great plan to break up our parents."

"Are you still on that idea?"

They looked at each other, and each of them raised an eyebrow.

"Anyway, this plan is really good." Brittany rubbed her hands together. "First I'm going to call my mom and tell her that Dad is dating a black woman. She'll call him in a heartbeat when she hears that."

Robyn scooted the chair closer to my bed. "When my mom finds out that Brittany's dad is talking to his ex-wife, she'll tell him he'd better make up his mind quick or she'll drop him. They'll be history for sure."

"Do you really think your dad will talk to your mom?" I asked Britt. Brittany's mom had been running around with a married man when I moved to Conyers, and filed for divorce shortly after. Brittany's dad hadn't spoken to her since.

"Well . . . she's kind of been sending him letters."

"What do you mean, kind of?"

"We wrote a couple of letters," Robyn explained, "and mailed them to him."

"You did what?" I shook my head. "Don't you think your dad will figure it out?"

"Maybe eventually," Brittany said. "But right now she's saying all the things he's waited years to hear. He's going to believe it because he wants to."

"That's sabotage!"

Brittany and Robyn went on and on about how they thought this was such a great idea. Neither of them saw anything immoral about it. They were telling me their plans like I was a part of their scheme. What did that say about me? They were planning to deceive their parents, and they expected me to pat them on their backs.

My Christian light might as well have not been shining

at all, because they certainly weren't seeing it. Christ would never do what they were suggesting. They were so engulfed with their own feelings they didn't care about how much they were going to hurt their parents.

When is it going to end? my conscience asked me. *When are you going to take a stand? Say something. If they don't listen to you, then distance yourself from this.*

I stood. "I don't want to hear any more. What you're doing is wrong." I looked at Brittany. "Your dad has really been hurt by your mom. What if your plan backfires? What if he gets in touch with your mom, and somehow they work things out because of some silly letters you wrote? Do you have any guarantee she'll really be committed to him? How bad will he feel if he gets rejected by her again? All those hopes and dreams will come crashing down even harder than the first time."

Brittany just rolled her eyes at me and looked out my window.

I turned to Robyn. "Your dad is gone. Just imagine him up in the heaven looking down on you. Do you think he'd be pleased with this scheme of yours?"

"Don't even go there, Laurel. I'm sure my dad would be upset about my mom making out with a white guy. My father worked hard to be one of the first African American airplane pilots. But because of his color they gave him the crummy flights on old planes. He flew three-leg flights in bad weather, and one of those flights took his life. So I don't think he'd be happy if he knew my mom was in the arms of the enemy."

I took a deep breath and asked the Lord for wisdom in answering her. "I don't know, Robyn, I think a lot of the stuff we hold on to down here doesn't really matter up in heaven. I'm sure your dad would want your mom to be with someone who really cares for her. You said it's tough when mixed-race couples go out on dates and people stare at them. Do you think your mom would put up with that if

141

she didn't have strong feelings for this guy? She's already been devastated by the death of her husband. What you're doing will just add more burden to her."

"What I'm doing is going to be better for her in the long run. You don't have the right to stand in my face to tell me what's best for my mom."

"Then don't tell me your business," I snapped back.

Brittany turned and stared at me.

"I love you guys, but I can't be your friend anymore. What you're doing to your parents is wrong and I don't want to be part of it. Get out of my house, and don't come back." I stormed out of my room, leaving the door open for them to show themselves out.

It wasn't easy telling them to remove themselves from my life, but as I did I could almost hear cheering from up above.

———————

After dinner that evening, Liam came up to me as I was doing the dishes. "I heard you tell your friends you didn't want to hang out with them anymore. I'm sorry."

Though Liam was younger than I was, he'd always been the strongest Christian of the four Shadrach children. He knew the Scriptures. He always did the right things, and for once I wasn't jealous of that. I used to hate that Liam made Dad so proud, but now I was proud of him too.

"I wish I could be the kind of Christian you are," I told him.

"I'm not perfect, either, so don't put me on a pedestal."

I knew he was right. None of us is going to be perfect until we're with God.

"But now that you're aware that your friends have been weighing you down, the Lord will hold you accountable to that. You can't compromise anymore. He can only get the glory when you do it His way. Look for friends who believe in Him. You did the right thing today."

I gave Liam a hug.

The next day my mom took me shopping to pick out stuff for my dorm room. Because she was even more perfect than Liam, I'd often found it hard to be myself around her. But now it was different. We laughed and joked, and talked about God's miracles.

"You know," I said as we were driving between Target and J C Penney, "I don't know if I'll make it on the University of Georgia gymnastics squad, but if God wants me there I'll be there. And if He doesn't, I know He has something else great for me. I'm just excited to give it my all and to give Him the glory for whatever He does."

She gave me a huge smile, and when we got to Penney's, she bought me everything I asked for. I felt good all over.

When I got home with my tons of bags, my brothers teased me.

"I'm sure when we go to college, we won't have twenty bags," Luke said.

I tried calling Branson again that night, but got his machine again. I really wanted to have a talk with him so we could figure out what was going on with us. We were about to go to the same college, so we at least needed to have some understanding in our relationship. But how could I meet with a guy who didn't want to meet with me?

I decided to visit Bo and see what he thought.

"What's on your mind?" he asked.

"Branson. Have you heard from him?"

"We talked."

"Then I guess you know the two of us are having some problems."

"No. Branson only talked about me and him."

"Oh. Well, what about you guys? Is he going to change his ways in order to hang out with you?"

"Unfortunately, no. He told me he wasn't ready for that. He didn't see himself getting close with the Lord anytime soon. He still has a lot of anger inside him."

"I'm sorry."

"Me too. But I'm not going to let him bring me down, even if that means I have to cut him loose."

My eyes stung with tears. I knew I had to do the same. God was giving me the confirmation I needed.

When I got back home, I tried Branson one more time. I couldn't believe he wasn't answering his phone.

Then I remembered Brittany told me about a party Jackson Reid was having that night. I knew Branson would be there. I asked my mom if I could borrow the car, and she said, "Fine, just be careful."

I drove around for a while just thinking. Was I really going to tell Branson it was over? How could I do that? Would I be jumping the gun? Was Branson really running in the opposite direction of God?

When I pulled up to Jackson's house, I saw Branson's car parked out front. I started feeling nervous. I knew there'd been booze and drugs at the party. I wondered what else I might encounter.

I threaded my way through the crowd, determined to find Branson, get this over with, and hightail it out of there. I found him . . . sitting in a corner of a back room with one girl running her fingers through his hair and another one kissing him in a way I wouldn't dare. It took every ounce of dignity I had to contain the tears. I just let the anger fuel my determination to stick with my decision and start ending the romance.

dealing
with sorrow

i stood in the hallway outside the back bedroom, unable to hold back the tears as I watched Branson making out with strangers. I wanted to run over there and hit him. Kick him. Tell him off. Something. But I just stood there crying. Because I wouldn't go all the way with him, was he going to use one of these bimbos to replace me?

Look at him, I told myself. *Look long and hard because you don't need to be in love with him anymore.*

Suddenly one of the girls stopped kissing Branson and stared at me. Branson followed her gaze, and the second he spotted me he rudely pushed her off him. As he came toward me, I realized I had nothing to say to him. His actions had said our good-byes clearly. I turned around quickly and scrambled for my car.

As soon as I got the engine revving, Branson started banging on the hood. He reached through the open window and grabbed my keys out of the ignition.

"Let me go," I said.

"No. We need to talk. I didn't mean for you to find out this way."

"What way? How long has this been going on? I called you several times. You've had every opportunity to tell me it was over between us, but you couldn't do that. You chickened out. I had to track you down. And it's a good thing I found you or I would have been in the dark about our relationship."

He backed away from the car, still holding my keys. I got out, but didn't follow him down the street.

"Branson, I'm not playing with you. Now, give me my keys." He was acting like we were in elementary school, and it made me angry. There was nothing he could say that would make me change my stance on wanting out of our relationship, so I didn't know why he was playing this game. After he got about ten feet away, he stopped walking and turned around, finally noticing that I wasn't behind him.

"I'm not chasing you down, Branson. You cheated on me because you don't want to be with me."

"That's not true," he said, strolling back toward me. "This reaction is what I've been waiting for. You came all the way out here to find me. You were in tears over me. That shows me you love me. I didn't want to be with those girls, but you made me think you didn't care about me. Now that I know you care, I really want you, Laurel."

"Yeah, I got that point a long time ago. But apparently what you really want is sex, with or without me." I snatched my keys out of his hands. "Well, you can play all your games without me. I'm living my life for God, Branson. There is no compromise, so go back to your party and have your fun."

I got in my car and slammed the door. Then I drove off. He ran after me for a few yards. Part of me wanted to stop the car and get out and hug him. But I couldn't do that. I was standing for God and He was going to give me strength. I'd gotten myself into this mess by falling in love with a nonbeliever. But before he made me fall any further, I needed to jump ship.

When I got home, I made myself a hot bath. I tried washing away my feelings for Branson. I scrubbed my body as if I were removing all the filth he'd placed into my brain. Then I laid the washcloth over my face, hoping that when I removed it, I would think, *Branson who?* But that didn't happen. I just felt more depressed. In the middle of my crying, someone knocked quietly on the bathroom door.

"Go away," I moaned.

"I need to talk to you," Lance said.

"I'm in the tub."

"You've been in there long enough. Come on."

He wasn't taking no for an answer. So I got out of the tub, put on my robe, and opened the door.

"OK, I'm out," I grumbled. "What's so important?"

"One of my friends just called. He told me you were at some party and you and Branson broke up."

It's all over town already? "And did your friend tell you why?" I asked.

"He said you saw Branson with some other girls."

"That's right," I said. "So what?"

Lance hesitated. "I guess I just want to say that maybe I haven't been the best brother to you I could be."

"This has nothing to do with you, Lance."

"I know you and Branson have been having problems for awhile, particularly in the area of sex. Laurel, girls come on to him all the time. I see it because I'm around him at football practice. He always takes their phone numbers. I told him that wasn't cool, but obviously it didn't do much good. He's a jerk, Laurel. He doesn't deserve you, even though I know you really like him. I know this is breaking your heart, but you did the right thing by walking away from him. He might have embarrassed you by being with those girls, but you got the last word. Everybody from the party is talking about how he got what he deserved. He's a laughingstock. I don't know if that gives you any consolation, but I wanted to tell you that."

Inwardly, it did help dry my tears.

"You're a good brother," I told him.

"I'm trying to be." He chuckled. "I know I've given you a hard time over the years, but I'm gonna miss you, Sis. When I grow up I want to be just like you."

"You kidder," I said as I tapped his chin.

Lance left so I could finish getting ready for bed. As I brushed my hair, I prayed. *Lord, thanks for showing me that I'm going to be fine without Branson. I love You, Lord. I love my family, and I love myself so much that I know I don't deserve to be with a guy who can't appreciate my worth. Thanks for helping me see that.*

"What are you guys doing here?" I said as I opened my front door the next day and saw Meagan, Brittany, and Robyn. Without a word, they passed me and let themselves in. I grabbed Meagan's arm. "You didn't tell me you were bringing anybody with you. I have nothing to say to those two."

"Well, we have something to say to you," Brittany replied.

"Then say it and leave."

"We know you and Branson broke up," Robyn said.

I wanted to scream, *"Does the world know?"*

"I'm OK, all right?"

Brittany snorted. "It's twelve o'clock and you're still in your pajamas. What are you doing? Sulking?"

"OK, so I'm not at my prettiest today. But I'm doing fine. And I don't need to discuss my personal life with you guys."

"Well, we've got some issues to discuss with you." Brittany went downstairs to the family room, with Robyn right behind her.

"I didn't want them here," I said to Meagan, "and I don't appreciate you tricking me."

"Come on, Laurel. Lighten up."

"That's the problem. I'm always letting everyone else run

my life. Well, not anymore. If you can't respect my wishes, then I'm going to have to cut you off just like I did them."

"They want to tell you they're sorry."

"Oh," I said. "Well, that's different."

I went downstairs to hear what my friends had to say. I felt extremely humbled. I had missed them. I was hurting and I needed my friends. I appreciated that they wanted to apologize.

But what did that really mean? There was a reason I'd cut ties with the two of them. Brittany and Robyn needed to understand that and change their hearts before I could change my mind about wanting to be their friend.

"You were right," Brittany said, her eyes red from crying. "My dad is so mad at me, he's shipping me away to college early. I have to leave next week to go live with my aunt down in Florida. Can you believe that? My dad said I broke his heart twice and he doesn't want to be around me."

"So your plan didn't work, huh?" I asked.

"Oh, it worked," Robyn said. "We broke our parents apart with our little scheme."

"What happened?"

Brittany sniffed. "My dad told Robyn's mom he had to cool down their relationship because he thought he might still have some feelings for his ex-wife. Of course that hurt Robyn's mom a lot. Those letters we wrote really got to my dad. They opened some old wounds, and he reached out to Mom. Of course, she had no idea what he was talking about when he mentioned the letters. She told him he needed to move on because she was engaged. He was devastated."

"My mom doesn't know I had a part in it yet," Robyn said. "Brittany's dad doesn't know I was in on it, either. But I feel bad because my mom hasn't had anyone interested in her in a long time."

"We were only thinking about ourselves," Brittany said. "And all along we had a good friend who tried to help us, but we ignored her advice."

"It's been hard not being able to talk to you about everything that's been going on in my life," Robyn said.

"And that goes double for me," Brittany agreed.

"That goes for me too," Meagan added.

"I'm not mad at you, Meg."

"Well, I called you a couple of times and you didn't call me back. When Britt told me why you were mad at her, I realized I haven't been a model Christian either. Maybe I don't lead you down the wrong path as much as she does, but I don't help you walk with God either. So I started asking God to change me."

"You did that because of me?"

"I need my friend Laurel," Meagan said. "My dad is planning to prosecute that fraternity house for what they did to me, and I'm going to have to give a deposition. I'm really nervous about my testimony, and I'd really like to have you around to hold my hand, pray for me, and give me the courage to face what I need to do. You're so strong, Laurel, and I know it's not because of you alone. I really see the Holy Spirit in you, and I want that for myself."

Brittany and Robyn nodded in heartfelt agreement.

I didn't even try to hold back my tears. The thought of anybody being able to see Christ in me was like a miracle in my life. Their words gave me encouragement to keep doing what I needed to. I had let my friends go, and they had come back saying they needed my help in their lives. They didn't want me to abandon them. They wanted me to show them the way.

"We'll all be going our separate ways pretty soon," I said, "so we don't have much time to spend together. How would you all like to spend the night?"

All night we talked about our issues, our burdens, our problems. We wrote them down and prayed that the Lord would take those burdens away, and in faith we believed that was going to happen. It was a joyous night. Our friendship was finally formed on a solid foundation. We were building on a solid rock.

Our problems hadn't gone away. I was still broken up with Branson. Meagan was still worried about testifying and reliving that horrible night. Brittany's dad was still mad at her. And Robyn's mom was still sad. But we had hope and we had each other. Those two great things gave us peace.

A few days later I was sitting in my room reading my newest Robin Jones Gunn novel when I heard feet shuffling in the hall. I glanced up and saw my youngest brother, Luke, standing at my bedroom door.

"Do you need something?" I asked.

"I just wanted to ask you a question."

I put a bookmark between the pages. "Is everything OK?"

He took a step inside. "I just wanted to know if you'd like to go to a movie with me."

"What time does it start?" I asked.

"In about forty-five minutes."

"I'd love to go with you. What are we seeing? You know what? I don't even care. I'm just glad to be hanging out with my little brother."

"Really?" he said.

My new godly attitude, combined with the knowledge that I'd be leaving home soon to head off for college, made me happy to spend what little time I had left with my family. Besides, Meagan and Brittany had gone to Florida, and Robyn had left for a vacation with her mom and her sister, Bunni. So I accepted my brother's invitation with great enthusiasm.

After the movies we went to Checkers and had banana splits.

"Do you think I'm a nerd?" he asked me.

"Why? Because you're smart? No, I think that's great. I wish I had your brains."

"You get good grades too," he said.

"Yeah, but I have to work hard to get them. It comes naturally to you." I scooped my spoon through the bowl, trying to get a little bit of all three topping flavors in one bite. "Why did you ask me that? What's going on with you?"

"Faigyn."

Foster's little sister and my youngest brother started seeing each other just before the shootout at school last fall. As a matter of fact, their feelings for each other had been the reason behind the tragedy, since the boy who started it all cared for Faigyn and saw how much she liked Luke.

"I've been meaning to ask you about her. Are you guys still together?"

"Sorta." He ate a big bite of ice-cream-covered banana before continuing his answer. "I bought a Christian journal for her, but I'm a little nervous about giving it to her. I haven't seen her all summer. Ever since the shooting it's been kind of weird between us. I don't know if she even likes me anymore."

"Sometimes girls want to be pursued," I told him. "Just because you've had a cold period, that doesn't mean she doesn't like you. Have you called her?"

Luke shook his head.

"You should. But don't just invite her to the movies. Get into God's Word with her. Pray with her. There are no promises that you'll marry her, but you can be her friend for life and her brother in Christ always. I'm sure that would mean a great deal to a young lady who's had a lot of turmoil in her life. I mean, having an ex-boyfriend try to kill you is pretty horrible. But having one who cares about your soul more than any part of your body is awesome."

I could tell he was soaking up every word I said. "Thanks, Sis."

Though my little brother was smarter than all three of us, he was still a little green. I felt like I was doing my last sisterly duty, where he was concerned, before I went off to school. It felt great.

But I also felt a little sad. I really loved my family and the thought of leaving them bothered me.

"Do you think we could go see her right now?" Luke asked.

I hesitated. I could tell my brother really wanted to see Faigyn. But going to her house meant we would probably see her brother, Foster.

I looked into Luke's pleading eyes, and couldn't say no.

We pulled up to their house just as Foster was getting ready to leave for the airport. My brother ran in to give Faigyn her present.

Foster smiled when he saw me, and I became a little emotional. "So, you're about to leave, huh?"

"Yeah. Was there something you wanted to tell me?" he asked.

"Yes, there is. You're a great guy, Foster McDowell, and you cut it off with me because I wasn't ready to stand where you stood in your walk with Christ. I will always admire you for that, and I'll never forget it because it changed me. I went back to something I thought was better, but somewhere along the way the example you set stood out in my mind and caused me to do the same thing."

He looked puzzled.

"I broke it off with Branson," I said.

"I heard about that."

"To be honest, it's been hard, but—" Tears stopped my words.

Foster gave me a friendly hug. "You're doing the right thing. Thanks for telling me that I did too. I mean, I knew that, but it's good to hear it before our paths go in different directions. I've been praying for you and I'll continue to do that. God's got an awesome plan for your life and He's got a special guy for you. I wish it could have been me, but He's got somebody for me too. Let's write each other, OK?" He gave me his school address.

"I don't know mine yet, but I'll give it to you when I write."

"I'm proud of you for taking a stand with Branson. I thought if anybody could change him, you could. He really did seem to care about you. But I'm glad you didn't change for him."

———————————

Two days later I had said good-bye to everyone except Branson. I knew our paths would probably cross at school, but until then I had to stay focused. My grandparents had flown out to see me off, so my folks planned a great meal.

After lunch, Derek started telling us what the summer had meant to him. "I've never had a dad. I mean, I have a father, but I never knew him. He didn't go to any of my football games or anything. He never asked me about my grades, women, or my walk with Christ. I didn't have a clue about what family functions were like. Seeing you guys, living with you and knowing what you mean to each other, has meant a lot to me. Now I want something greater for my life. I want to be a strong, godly man, and I pray that the Lord will give me a wife and children so I can make an impact on this world with my family like you, Rev. Shadrach. Since Laurel is about to leave, I'd like to encourage you all to open up and say what's on your hearts while you've got the chance."

Everyone took turns saying how much I meant to them. I responded by saying, "I love you all too. And even though I won't be with you in this house, you will all be with me in my heart. Dad, I'll hear your voice telling me what's right and wrong. Mom, I'll hear you whispering guidance into my ear. And I'll hear my brothers saying the nutty things you always say. I'll feel the prayers of my grandparents. And thanks to you, Derek, I'll never take my family for granted again because I saw them through your eyes."

"Why are you crying?" Luke asked.

"They're tears of joy," I said, "and believe it or not, I'm enjoying dealing with sorrow."

choosing my way

my parents had been waiting on me for two hours, but every time I thought I was ready I remembered something else I needed to take or something I wasn't sure I'd packed. When my mom opened the front door and asked me one more time if I was ready, I said, "You know what? I'm not. I've changed my mind. I don't want to go to college. I thought I was ready to be on my own, but I was wrong."

Mom held my hand and tugged me down to the floor. We knelt together and she prayed.

"Lord, my daughter is having a case of the jitters here. It's time for her to go off to college, but she doesn't want to leave the nest. A part of me doesn't want her to go either. But I know there's no need for either of us to fear because You're with us always and You know how to care for what belongs to You. My daughter is Your child. You've given her to me for all these years, and I'm thankful for that. But now it's time for her to fly on her own. Help her, Lord, to know that You're going to be with her, and remind her that we're just forty-five miles away if she needs us. Now is not the time for her to change her mind. Help her to build her future beyond these walls and to live out Your purpose for her life. Help her to make wise choices, Lord."

My mom stopped and sniffled, so I continued. "Lord, bless my mom. Help her be strong while I'm away. Thank You, Lord, for giving me such great parents. Give them peace and comfort. And give me strength. I'm a little nervous right now, but talking to You helps me regain my focus. Thank You, Lord. Amen."

We squeezed each other's hands and stood. "I'm ready to go now," I said. "I think I have everything I need."

My dad drove the family van so all three of my brothers could ride along. The car was quiet. No one talked. I didn't want my last few moments with them to be like a funeral. I had to break the ice. I wanted to make the ride fun. So I started singing "My Favorite Things" from *The Sound of Music.* After every verse I said, "I love you guys."

When we entered the Athens city limits, I saw a Cracker Barrel restaurant. That was one of my favorite places to eat, so I pointed it out.

"Are you guys hungry already?" Dad asked.

My mother had just fed us a great lunch, but no one wanted to say good-bye yet. "I bet they've got blackberry cobbler," Mom suggested.

They did, and it was scrumptious. "Hey, why don't you guys all give me some last-minute advice."

"You never want to hear what we have to say," Lance teased.

"I know. But forget the past. I'm asking for some now. Everybody tell me something. Not a whole paragraph, but something quick."

Luke started off. "Don't party too hard, but study real hard."

My dad bopped him on the head. "She'd better not be partying at all."

"I think you should go to the parties," Lance said. "That's where you'll meet new friends. Enjoy college. Have fun. Just be sure it's the right kind of fun."

Liam said, "Like the song we were just singing, whenever life gets tough and things aren't going the way you want, remember the good stuff. Like your family."

My mom said, "Remember our prayer. No matter what, God is always there."

"All good advice," my dad said. "Well, some of it," he added, grimacing at Lance. "Whatever you do, wherever you go, be a light. Keep choosing God daily. Listen to the Holy Spirit. You're going to be tested in college. You thought your high school years were crazy. Get ready for a lot more. You can handle it only if you let God lead, and if you follow nothing else but Him."

As we left the restaurant, Mom told Liam to get in the front so she could sit beside me. I leaned my head on her shoulder.

"There it is," Liam said as we approached my new home.

As my brothers unloaded my stuff I felt my knees getting weak.

"Baby," Dad said, "I'm proud of you." He handed me a checkbook.

"Dad!"

"There's three thousand dollars in the account. Manage it wisely. We don't want you to have to work this year. We'd rather you concentrate on school." My dad started getting all choked up.

"Don't cry," I said.

"I wish I could give you a car."

"Dad, your prayers for me are worth more than a car any day."

My family helped carry my bags to the main entrance, but dorm rules wouldn't allow my brothers past the lobby. So Mom and Dad and I toted my bags down the hall to my first-floor dorm room.

"Looks like you already have a roommate," Mom said as we stepped through the open door.

Please, Lord, I prayed, *let her know You.*

"She has nice taste," Mom said, checking out the maroon comforter on the bed farthest from the door. She opened one of the closet doors. "She's neat too. Good sign."

"Mom!"

As I dumped my bags onto the floor by the empty closet, I called out, "Hello? Is anybody here?"

A girl came out of the bathroom. To my great surprise she was black. I don't know why I thought black people wouldn't go to this school. I guess I just wasn't thinking. She was really pretty. Beautiful brown skin and a pleasant smile. But she seemed nervous. Maybe she'd wanted a black roommate.

She lingered in the bathroom doorway, so I went up to her. "I'm Laurel Casey Shadrach," I said, holding out my hand to her. "I'm from Conyers."

"Hi," she said, shaking my hand. "I'm Payton Autumn Skyy."

"What a lovely name," Mom said. "Where are you from?"

"Augusta, ma'am," my new roommate said.

I grinned, knowing how impressed Mom would be with being called "ma'am."

"Well, Payton from Augusta," Dad said, "it's lovely to meet you." His eyes glanced at the Bible on the desk beside the maroon-covered bed. "Laurel, seems like you were blessed with a pretty nice young lady for a roommate. I know you gals are going to get along just fine."

My dad gave me a short pep talk about how we should look out for each other. Then he said they'd better get back to my brothers. They wished my new roommate the best and started to leave.

"Let me walk you to the door," I suggested.

"No, you stay and get to know your new roommate," Mom said. "You already said good-bye to everyone. We'll call you when we get home."

The minute the door closed, I flopped onto the bed. All the tears I'd been holding back finally fell. Payton handed me a tissue.

"Thanks," I said. "I'm not usually such a big baby."

"Don't worry. I did the same thing about an hour ago."

"Maybe there's hope for me then," I said with a small smile.

We talked while Payton helped me get my side of the room together. It turned out we had a lot in common. She was the oldest in her family. She had a younger brother named Perry, who was two years younger that she, the same age as Lance. And she had two ex-boyfriends going to Georgia.

I laughed. "And I thought I had problems with just one." I told her about Branson, and how he didn't make it on the football team because of an injury.

"My guys are both on the team," Payton said. "They're battling over the same spot: starting tailback."

I told Payton about my girlfriends and my family.

"Hey, you want to pray?" I suggested.

She nodded, and we bowed our heads. But before we could really get started, I heard loud voices coming from the bathroom.

"What's that?" I asked.

"We share a bathroom with two other girls."

"Really?" I wasn't really excited about the prospect of sharing a bathroom with three girls. Sharing with three brothers had been bad enough. I sighed and continued the prayer.

Just after I said "amen," a female voice said "amen," too, with a Southern drawl.

I opened my eyes and saw a slightly overweight girl with very curly strawberry blond hair standing at the bathroom door. She looked rather plain, but with a little bit of makeup I could tell she would be beautiful.

"I'm Anna," she said in a cute country voice.

Before we could say anything, Anna was distracted by a noise from the other room. "What are you doing?" Anna shouted. "Put my stuff back on the bed."

Payton and I followed Anna through the bathroom and into the adjoining room. There I saw a very cute redhead. Her mid-length hair looked like Meagan's, but her attitude reminded me of Brittany. I could tell from all her trunks she had money.

"I don't want to be on this side," the red-haired girl screeched. "I'm moving my stuff to the other side."

"You can't do that, Jewels," Anna said. "I was here first. My stuff is already set up." Anna threw Jewels's stuff on the floor.

I thought these two girls were going to get into a fist fight, so I tried to be a peacemaker. "Hey, guys, there's got to be a way to work this out."

Jewels glared at Payton and me. "You two just worry about what happens on your side of the bathroom and not about what goes on over here."

Payton stepped in. "Well, if you two would talk to each other with some respect, and not yell and scream so we could hear you from our side of the room, we wouldn't have to be in your business. We came over here so we can all get along, since we're all sharing a bathroom."

"That doesn't mean we have to share the same space," Jewels said. "When you're in there, I won't be."

"Fine, then," Payton said. "Let me get out of your space right now." She stormed out of the room.

I started to follow her, but Jewels said, "Wait. Stay and talk to us. Are you doing the sorority thing?"

I couldn't believe how quickly this ranting girl could

switch to sounding so sweet. But I figured it would be a good idea to try to make friends with her. "I'm planning on checking it out. My mom's an Alpha Gamma."

"My mom was, too, and my sister still is. That's my first choice. Anna and I are planning to pick up the sorority information, and then we're going to grab a bite to eat. You want to join us?"

"Maybe. Let me see what my roommate wants to—"

"Come on. She doesn't need you to hold her hand."

Jewels was being pushy, but a quick glance into my room told me that Payton had left. So I gave in, hoping I wouldn't regret it.

"Why didn't we just go to the cafeteria?" I asked Jewels and Anna as they drove around trying to find a restaurant they liked.

"My sister says no one eats at the cafeteria," Jewels bragged.

I didn't want to blow my dad's checking account money on food. I had a cafeteria card, so that was where I planned on eating, even if I was the only one.

"Surely somebody eats there."

"Yeah," Jewels replied. "Losers!" She pulled her brand-new Ford Mustang into a Red Lobster parking lot.

"I don't think I can afford this," I said.

"It's crowded anyway," Anna said. "Let's go to the Cracker Barrel."

"I will not go there," Jewels said with disgust.

Though I had just eaten there with my family, I could do it again. "I think it's a great idea."

After giving me a sideways glance, Jewels reluctantly drove out of the Red Lobster parking lot and down the street toward the Cracker Barrel.

As we got out of the car, I saw my family's van pulling out of the parking lot. I ran up to it and my dad parked in the nearest space. Everyone tumbled out of the car.

"What are you guys doing here?" I asked.

Lance chuckled. "We got halfway home and Luke realized he'd left his wallet here. So we came back, and then we decided to eat dinner."

"How'd you get here?" my mom asked.

"I rode with my new suite mates, Anna and Jewels." I turned around and found them standing right behind me. I introduced my new friends to my family.

Jewels told my mom that her mother was also an Alpha Gamma. She complimented my brothers on how handsome they were. Her model-citizen act made me want to vomit.

"So, Laurel, this must be your older brother," she said, eyeing my dad.

When he started to blush, my mom elbowed him in the side.

"That's my father, Reverend Shadrach," I corrected her.

"Reverend!" She instantly dropped the flirting. "You don't have to worry about Laurel, sir. I'll make sure she does what she's supposed to."

If she's going to be watching over me, I'll probably be expelled in a week, I thought.

Dad gave me a twenty-dollar bill and told us to have dessert on him. I hugged him and kissed him. "I'm going to miss you guys," I said for the zillionth time that day.

"Well, it looks like you've met some pretty nice young ladies," Dad said.

I wanted to thank the Lord for allowing me one more chance to see my family, but I wasn't sure it was a good thing. I mean, I was about to cry all over again when I saw them pull out of the restaurant and head toward Conyers.

Anna took my hand. "Come on. Let's eat."

As we had dinner, Anna talked about her fears, which were very similar to mine. Jewels just laughed at us. When Anna mentioned that she was self-conscious, and she didn't like her parents, and she hated being from a single-parent home, Jewels smirked. I wanted to strangle her.

I told Anna that my dad was a pastor, and that made things difficult for me sometimes. Before I could say anything else, Jewels started bragging about how great her life was.

"My dad is a builder. I have one older sister, named Julie Anne. Georgia wasn't my first choice, but since it's where my parents and my sister went to school, I got a new car when I agreed to come here." The more she talked, the more I knew she was not my kind of friend. But I realized college would introduce me to all kinds of people, and they wouldn't all be my type.

When Jewels stopped talking long enough to take a sip of her soda, I said, "You know, Anna, there are things I don't like about myself." She looked at me like she wanted me to name one. "But I don't like going into negatives because I prefer to focus on the positives. That's why we're in school, to become the best women we can be. We all have room to grow," I said, glancing at Jewels. "So don't worry about who you are today. Look forward to who you're going to be tomorrow."

Anna smiled for the first time all evening. "Hey," she said, "Would you like to go to a freshman party with us? The fraternities and sororities are having a mixer tonight for all the new people interested in pledging."

"Sounds great," I said.

When we got back to the dorm to change for the party, I heard screaming and yelling. Then I recognize Payton's voice. I opened the door to my room, but Payton was nowhere in sight. I could still hear her hollering, so I checked the bathroom. Anna checked the closet.

Jewels pulled back the curtain and looked out the window. "Come here and look at this."

I peeked over her shoulder and saw two black guys in the yard, fighting. Payton was standing there screaming.

"Man, I told you to leave her alone," the darker guy said, his hand around the other guy's throat.

"What are they doing?" Anna said.

"Look at that guy's thighs," Jewels said.

As the argument got louder and more heated, people started gathering around.

"You two have to stop," Payton cried. "This is crazy."

"See what you're doing, man?" the darker guy said. The other one socked him in the stomach, then went over to Payton.

"Get away from me, Dakari," she said.

I recognized the name from our talk that afternoon. Dakari was the boyfriend Payton had told me about who dumped her at the beginning of the year for some new girl at school.

"Tad, no!" Payton yelled as the other guy pushed Dakari against our window. Anna and Jewels and I jumped back from the impact. Dakari managed to turn things around so Tad's back was up against the window. Then Dakari pulled back his fist, but Tad moved his head at the last second and Dakari's fist went straight through the glass.

"Payton, what's going on?" I screamed out the broken window.

"Get me a towel," she hollered, stooping to check Dakari's hand.

I grabbed one of the maroon towels from our bathroom and tossed it out the broken window to her. Tad tried to wrap it around Dakari's bleeding hand, but Dakari lashed back at him.

Before the two of them could get into another brawl, the campus police showed up. Two uniformed officers took both guys away in a squad car.

"Well, that was interesting," Jewels said, heading back to her room. "We'd better hurry up and get ready for that party. We have to leave in twenty minutes."

I wanted to scream. "You guys go ahead. I'm not going to be ready on time."

"Whatever," Jewels grumbled from the other side of our suite.

I rushed outside to try to help Payton. But I couldn't find her anywhere. So I went back to the room, stopping at the resident assistant's room to get a broom, dustpan, masking tape, and a roll of cellophane. I picked up all the big pieces of broken glass and tossed them into the wastebasket, then swept up the rest and poured them in too. I covered the window with the cellophane, affixing it to the window frame with plenty of masking tape.

After returning the supplies, I checked outside again. I still saw no sign of Payton.

At that moment, I knew what the Lord wanted me to do, and I was determined to do it. On my very first day at school, I could clearly see the walk God wanted me to walk, and I was choosing His way.

understanding
what counts

a s I started to walk back into the dorm, I heard snicker-ing from four white girls who were pointing at the broken window. I remembered seeing them in the crowd watching Tad and Dakari fight. So I strolled up to them and said, "Hi."

"Hi," they said back, still giggling.

"You guys, that was my roommate, Payton Skyy. I don't really know her yet, but she's really hurting. Do you think you could give her a break and not laugh at her painful situation?"

"Sure," one said.

"We were about to go inside anyway," another added.

"What's your name?" a third girl asked.

We all introduced ourselves, and I found out that these girls lived on the fourth floor.

"This dorm is bad luck now," one of the girls said.

"Bad luck?" I asked.

"Oh, yeah," she said. "If something really dramatic happens on the first day, it's a bad sign."

"I'm a Christian," I told her. "I believe that God controls things. He can do whatever He wants. There's no such thing as luck."

"I hope you're right," she said as they walked away.

When I returned to my room, I was surprised to see Anna and Jewels still there.

"So, are you ready to go?" Jewels asked.

"I told you guys you could go without me."

"We didn't want to," Anna said. "We heard you talking to those girls outside. That was really nice."

"It was cool of you to fix the window too," Jewels added.

"So we figured we could wait for you. If you hurry up and get dressed, we can still all go together."

"Give me five minutes," I said.

They closed the door and I searched my closet for the right thing to wear.

Lord, I prayed as I got dressed, *I don't know what's waiting for me at this party, but I know the only way I can survive is if You come with me. Please make me light in the darkness.*

I stared at myself in the mirror. *I look cute,* I thought, a little surprised. And it wasn't just my adorable dress. I could see the Holy Spirit inside me, shining brightly. I didn't have to go anywhere alone because I was one with God.

I went through the bathroom to join my suite mates in their room. Jewels was fixing Anna's hair. "I just don't think having a black roommate will help me get into one of the more prestigious sororities," Jewels said.

"You're probably right," Anna agreed.

"That is so racist," I said.

Jewels and Anna turned around, obviously just noticing that I had joined them.

"It's not just the fact that she's black," Jewels said. "Look at the kind of people she hangs out with. Those boyfriends of hers were fighting like animals."

"You can take people out of the ghetto," Anna said, "but you can't take the ghetto out of people."

I stared at them, unable to come up with a good response.

"Maybe you should start looking for a new roommate, Laurel," Anna suggested. "I mean, your reputation could be damaged. Besides, you don't want to room with someone who can't understand who you are."

"Are either of you guys Christians?" I asked.

"I'm Catholic," Anna said.

"What does being a Christian have to do with anything?" Jewels asked. "We're talking about getting into a sorority, not heaven. That roommate of yours is going to ruin all of our chances. Since you kinda made friends with her, maybe you can tell her in a nice way to move out and find a different room."

"I'm not going to do that," I said, angry that she would even think such a thing.

Jewels glared at me. "If you can't ask her nicely, I'll just tell her to get out."

I took a deep breath to calm my emotions. "I want to pledge to a sorority too. Alpha Gamma is my first choice, but if that doesn't work out, it's OK. Showing Christ's love to people is far more important. And to be honest, I'd rather be Payton's roommate than yours any day."

Jewels and Anna stared at me with their mouths open.

I was on a roll. I could feel God speaking to them through me, so I kept going. "Payton needs a friend right now. If you guys aren't up for it, that's fine, but I am. And don't tell me what's good for me because you don't know the same God I do."

I turned around and stormed back to my room. When I tromped through the bathroom doorway, I saw Payton sitting on her bed, tears streaming down her cheeks.

"Did you hear all that?" I asked.

She nodded.

I sat beside her. "Payton, you do know the God I know, and He can give you the strength to face the tough stuff. It wasn't easy telling those girls over there that I don't care what they think. A couple of years ago, I wouldn't have been able to say that. Back then, I didn't let the power inside me work, but it's working now. I'm still struggling in some areas. Believe me, I've got problems. But when I tap into the Holy Spirit and let His light shine, I amaze myself sometimes."

Payton shot looks of hatred through the bathroom at our suite mates. "I can't stand those two girls," she seethed.

"I understand how you feel. But I'm not going to give up on Jewels and Anna. There's something wrong with the way they perceive stuff, but they need to know about God too. Until they do, we have to help them."

"I know you're right," Payton said, calming down a bit. "Thanks for straightening me out." She looked into the other room, this time with sadness. "And thanks for sticking up for me in there."

I smiled. "We've got to encourage each other. I'm sure there's going to be a time when I need you to stick up for me."

We gave each other a hug. "I still want to go to that sorority mixer," I said. "You want to come?"

"No," she said, wiping her eyes. "I think I'll stay here. Tad or Dakari might call."

I prayed with her, then joined Anna and Jewels next door.

"Is she OK?" Anna asked.

"She will be," I said with confidence.

The outdoor block party had tons of people milling around, and one of the first ones I saw was Branson Price. Why did he look so good? He wore a white tank top and his muscles bulged out in all the right places. I wanted to go up to him and say, *"Hey, here I am! The one who loves you."* But I did a quick reality check and started walking through the crowd, far away from him.

"Wait," Jewels said. "Why are you walking so fast? We've got to check out these sororities." She flipped through several brochures. "This one looks like the most elite," she said, pointing to one, "because they only take girls who have really high GPAs. But that one," she said, pointing to a different brochure, "says they have the most girls who become homecoming queen."

Maybe this isn't for me after all, I thought.

I kept walking with Jewels, and gradually her voice faded. When I turned around she was gone. After a quick look, I found her. She was standing five feet away from me, talking to Branson. She was twirling her hair with her fingers and swaying her hips. If I stood back and did nothing a few seconds longer, I figured the two of them might become an item. So I took a deep breath and strode up to them.

"You have a girlfriend?" I heard Jewels say as I stepped closer. "No freshman comes to college already attached."

"There she is," he said, looking my way.

Jewels turned. "Where? I don't see anybody." She was looking me right in the eye. Obviously she didn't think this fine guy could possibly be talking about me. And I couldn't believe he was referring to me as his girlfriend.

"Hi, Laurel." Branson planted a kiss on my cheek.

"This is your girlfriend?" Jewels asked. "Did you know she's a Christian, and her dad's a pastor? She seems way too stuffy for you."

"Jewels, could we have some space?" I said.

"Fine, fine, fine." She turned to Branson. "We're suite mates, so if things don't work out between you guys, you know where to find me."

"Jewels!"

She shrugged and sauntered off.

"So I see you've already made some friends here," Branson said. His eyes looked bloodshot and he stumbled over his words.

"What's going on with you?" I asked. I didn't smell any alcohol on his breath, nor did I get any hint of mint cover-up.

"Laurel," he said, "our whole town is laughing at me because of what you did. At first I was pretty mad at you. But then I realized I had it coming for making out with other girls. I'm sorry about that."

He was saying the things I wanted to hear, but something wasn't right. He was different somehow, and not in a good way.

"Why aren't you saying anything, Laurel? Didn't you miss me too?"

He reached out to hug me. I tried to get away, but wasn't fast enough. He swooped me up in his arms. Though I couldn't place the aroma, he smelled a little funny. Then some guy I'd never seen bumped into us.

"There you are, man. I been looking all over for you. Hey, I see you found a babe. Well, bring her along. I don't wanna smoke this alone."

I pushed Branson off of me. "Have you been using drugs?"

He blinked at me. His friend chuckled.

"What do you take me for? Coming on to me like you missed me when you're not even thinking clearly. This is insulting, Branson." I started to storm off, but he grabbed my arm.

"Wait!" he called.

"Get off me." I pulled my arm out of his grasp. "And get off the drugs. You think you're so hip. Well, your fancy words won't work this time. You haven't changed."

"Are you gonna let her talk to you like that?" the jerk with the drugs asked.

Branson looked around and noticed a crowd had started watching us. I didn't care, but I could tell he was embarrassed.

His face turned red and he threw his hands up. "Forget you!"

I let him have what was left of his pride and watched him walk away.

"You're so judgmental," Jewels said, sidling up to me. "You shouldn't get on his case about partying. It's only a matter of time before you have some fun yourself."

I knew she was right. I was hanging out in the same scene, which made me no better than Branson. Sure, I hadn't yielded to temptation yet, but it was all around me. I felt like a hypocrite.

"I'll see you back at the dorm," I told her.

"You shouldn't walk around campus alone."

"I'll be OK," I grumbled.

I didn't mean to snap at her, but I had issues to deal with. I'd been telling Payton what she should do, and now I was telling Branson, when I really needed to look at myself.

A girl who looked a little older than I stopped me as I started to pass her. "Hi, I'm Liza. I'm the pledge master for from Alpha Gam, and I wanted to tell you I was really impressed by what you said to that guy. All the other sororities and fraternities are into crazy stuff, but we at Alpha Gam are about community service and enjoying our college years in legal ways. You're somebody I'd really like to have in our organization. I hope you'll consider Alpha Gam."

"Thanks," I said to her. She had me intrigued, but at the moment I just wanted to get back to my dorm room.

All the way back, I thought I heard footsteps following me. I kept looking around, but didn't see anything suspicious.

I have to get it together.

I concentrated on the beautiful Georgia sky. It was dark purple and filled with twinkling stars. I felt like angels were up there winking at me, telling me, "It's going to be OK. We're up here watching you."

I got to my new home safely, but I vowed to God that I

would not do that again. On the way down the hall to my room, I prayed for Branson and for Payton. I also prayed for Payton's ex-boyfriends, Tad and Dakari.

Payton wasn't in the room when I got there. I hoped she was OK. I took a shower, then wrapped my wet hair in a towel, put on my bathrobe, and relaxed on the bed. I turned on my Christian music softly, happy to have a moment of peace.

I hadn't been perfect that day, but I wasn't the weak girl I used to be. I could see myself growing, and that gave me peace.

I woke up to someone shaking me.

"We need to talk." Jewels stood over me like an old mother hen.

"What time is it?" I asked.

"Ten o'clock. Why?"

"I thought you guys were going to be at the party all night."

"I planned to, but then my sister told me the sororities want their potential pledges not to stay out late. Some old-fashioned thing about good girls being in before ten. So here we are. But come on. We have some things to talk about."

She grabbed my arm and yanked me all the way to her side of the suite.

"Ow," I said.

Jewels plopped me down on her bed beside Anna. "I just want to tell you that I'm sorry I called you judgmental."

She didn't really sound apologetic. It seemed to me she was just doing it because she had to.

"So, what's so important that you had to drag me all the way over here?"

"My sister told me a lot of her sorority sisters thought you were really impressive standing up to that guy. The word is, the Alpha Gams really want you. When I mentioned to my sister that your father was a pastor, she said they really, really want you. I guess a girl who just graduated had a dad who was a pastor, and he used to come up here and do programs for them, and pray for their sorority, and counsel the girls. Now they don't have that anymore, so they feel like they could use you."

"Really?" I said.

"There was one thing they thought was kind of bad, though."

"*They* didn't think that," Anna corrected. "Just your sister."

Jewels glared at Anna. "They're not even into you, so just hush."

Anna looked dejected, and I felt bad for her.

"Anyway, my sister thought that you rooming with an African American girl wasn't . . . you know . . ."

She didn't finish her sentence, but I knew what she was implying.

"Most of the sororities like for their girls to room with other girls from the same sorority."

"That part is true," Anna said.

"I just think we'd all have a better chance if you got another roommate. It wouldn't be that hard. You don't have to say you want to switch rooms because she's black. Just make up something. Payton seems really down anyway. She might want to room with a girl who can understand her culture."

I stared at Jewels, unable to believe what I was hearing. "Let me tell you something," I said, standing. "I would rather room with a Christian girl, regardless of her color, than someone who doesn't know the Lord." I said it in a sweet but firm way, and their mouths dropped open. "Good night." I grabbed the doorknob and twisted it, but my door wouldn't open. I pushed harder and I found Payton on the other side in tears.

"You don't have to room with me," she said.

"Didn't you hear what I told them?" I said, leading her to

174

the bed. "Payton, one of my best girlfriends in high school was a black girl. Her name is Robyn. I helped her get through some really difficult times. I had to stop being her friend for awhile because she and my other friend, Brittany, were doing stupid stuff over race issues. But God allowed them to come back to me." I took Payton's brown hand in my white one. "You are a far better roommate than those white girls next door could ever be. Jewels thinks she has everything, and Anna is desperately hoping to get something. What they both need is Jesus Christ in their hearts."

Payton choked back a sob. She didn't seem ready to talk, so I continued. "You and I can help each other. We're family because we're sisters in Christ."

She gave me a hug.

"All of our problems have already been answered at the Cross. Jesus Christ died for our sins. As long as we're connected to Him, we have no worries, no fear, no problems, no doubts, and no anxiety because the price for all of that was paid on Calvary. All we have to do is believe it and run to Him every time. Run to Him for strength, guidance, joy, help, and peace."

Though I hadn't taken one college class yet, I was already learning great lessons. Life wasn't about being black or white, or rich or poor. It was about being rich in the Word of God and being cleansed by the blood of Jesus.

While Payton took a shower, I grabbed the Bible off my nightstand. I read the passage about being equally yoked, and I knew God was showing me through His Word that I needed to be equally yoked in all areas of my life. I had to bind myself together with people who believed the same things I did. I needed people who loved God to help me live more like Christ.

I closed the Bible and crossed over to the window, which had been fixed as good as new. I opened it and looked outside, smelling the sweet night air. The sky was beautiful and peaceful. The stars, my angels, were still up there twinkling at me. I thanked God for helping me to stand for Him, even in tough times. I didn't know what might happen next in my life, but I knew God was going to walk the next step with me. My life was great because I belonged to the King. I was finally understanding what counts.

S INCE 1894, Moody Publishers has been dedicated to equip and motivate people to advance the cause of Christ by publishing evangelical Christian literature and other media for all ages, around the world. Because we are a ministry of the Moody Bible Institute of Chicago, a portion of the proceeds from the sale of this book go to train the next generation of Christian leaders.

If we may serve you in any way in your spiritual journey toward understanding Christ and the Christian life, please contact us at www.moodypublishers.com.

"All Scripture is God-breathed and is useful for teaching, rebuking, correcting and training in righteousness, so that the man of God may be thoroughly equipped for every good work."
                                        —*2 TIMOTHY 3:16, 17*

Laurel Shadrach Series

Purity Reigns

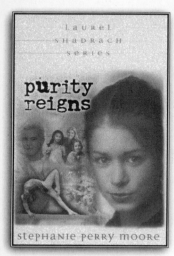

Laurel Shadrach is looking forward to her senior year being picture perfect! However, when Branson begins to pressure her in their relationship, Laurel is faced with making a choice between obeying God and giving in to the desires of her flesh..

Will the pressure she feels from Branson destroy her relationships with her Father, family and friends? Will Laurel have the courage to say no to the man she loves?

ISBN: 0-8024-4035-5

Totally Free

Laurel finds herself dealing with the effects of alcohol abuse on friends, family, and a community; a brother who is controlled by the excitement of gambling; and the peer pressures of giving in to sexual urges. Will Laurel continue to bear this heavy burden of secrecy and tolerance alone? Will the Lord show Himself faithful even in these difficult situations?

ISBN: 0-8024-4036-3

ISBN: 0-8024-4038-X

Absolutely Worthy

Laurel's roommate, Payton Skky, is also a believer and a welcome friend. When Laurel decides to rush the Alpha Gams with Jewels, her friend, she has some choices to make about her personal conduct, her true friendships, and her gymnastics future.

Will Laurel come to realize her true identity in Christ?

Finally Sure

Laurel Shadrach begins her second semester as a University of Georgia freshman with two clouds hanging over her head. First, her grandfather is dying, and second she is in danger of being cut from the gymnastics team, which means she'll lose the scholarship money that would keep her at the
prestigious university.

The semester is destined to be one of victories and defeats for Laurel.

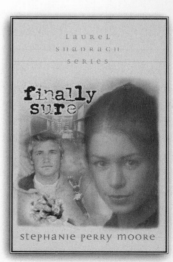

ISBN: 0-8024-4039-8

MOODY
PUBLISHERS

THE NAME YOU CAN TRUST.

1-800-678-6928 www.MoodyPublishers.org

EQUALLY YOKED TEAM

ACQUIRING EDITOR
Greg Thornton

COPY EDITOR
Kathy Ide

BACK COVER COPY
Julie-Allyson Ieron, Joy Media

COVER DESIGN
Ragont Design

INTERIOR DESIGN
Ragont Design

PRINTING AND BINDING
Bethany Press International

The typeface for the text of this book is
Berkeley